"La merde has just frapped le fan!" RCMP Inspector "Rocky" Glen Acorn, not one to horse around, tore into Constables Kerr and Potts, who stood at attention in his office. "Your arses are in a sling. We just made the biggest marijuana bust in local history, got great publicity for it, and you two let some gang of stick-up artists steal nearly half a million bucks worth of prime BC pot that you were supposed to be guarding. You've made the Force a laughingstock in the War on Drugs!"

"We had to stop," Potts explained. "They were blocking the road."

"Two women," Acorn put in. "And I'll bet these weren't bag ladies, were they? Drop-dead babes in the woods, I'll wager. And maybe you thought you could score. Right?"

"The thought might have crossed our minds, sir," Kerr admitted.

> "Read no more than two chapters at a time or
> you could bust a gut laughing."
> – *Pat Macdonald, poet laureate of Edmonton*

Also by Hal Sisson

Published by Global Outlook
Modus Operandi 9/11

Published by Salal Press
You Should Live So Long
Maquiladora Mayhem
Fat Lot of Good
A Fowler View of Life
The Big Bamboozle

(with Dwayne Rowe)
Garage Sale of the Mind
Coots, Codgers and Curmudgeons
(originally published by Orca Books)

Published by Arsenal Pulp Press
Caverns of the Cross

Published by Llumina Press
Sorry 'Bout That

To the millions of people who have been
illegally and immorally harassed or
incarcerated for possessing, using or
growing hemp by the agencies
carrying out the corrupt, useless and stupid
War on Drugs. Likewise for those
involved in prostitution. Prohibition doesn't
work in either case; never has, never will.

And to the people who carry notebooks or
use scraps of papers to write down
interesting bits they hear and see around them,
in order to preserve and pass them on
for the enjoyment of others.

ACKNOWLEDGEMENTS

Thanks to two friends with a great sense of humour, namely Pat Macdonald, the "poet laureate of Edmonton" for his raunchy joke poems, and Glen Acorn, who actually has siblings named Ivan and Hazel. And thanks to Wayne Halyn, nifty name expert.

A grateful nod as well to Mark Twain, who heard an inmate of a mental institution remark: "Forgiveness is the fragrance the violet sheds on the heel that crushed it," and passed on that gem.

I've also been inspired by a myriad of writers and joke compilers who made me laugh: guys like G. Legman, author of The Rationale of the Dirty Joke, Benny Hill, Hal Roach, Jim Pietsch, Richard Lederer, Louis A. Safian, Fred Metcalf, Jon Winoker, Robert Byrne, Leonard Levinson, Spike Milligan, Ambrose Bierce, Ken Smith, Jonathan Green, Bob Hope, J.P. Donleavy, and so many, many others.

Did you hear the one about the old Irishman who was dying? The doctor told him he wouldn't live to see the next day's sunrise. The Irishman's wife went up to the bedroom and said to him, "Dear old husband, this is your last night on Earth. Have you any last request?"

The old man whispered: "I can smell that you're cooking one of your fine Irish stews down in the kitchen. I'd like you to bring me a bowl of that stew."

"You can't have any," said the wife. "I'm cooking the stew for tomorrow's wake."

Dead on the Level

The reason Santa Claus is always so jolly is because he knows where all the bad girls live. Santa no doubt knew where Dusty Rhodes and Thistle Fielgud were temporarily living in late December of 1986.

As active founding members of the Naughty But Nice, Inc. escort service (their motto being: Take a walk on the wild side and taste the forbidden fruit), they had booked a room at the Dominion Hotel in downtown Victoria, British Columbia. The hotel hosted groups of party-loving conventioneers on a regular basis.

The Naughty girls had staked out their respective territories, but would switch locales from time to time. They worked in pairs to keep tabs on each other's activities and in case they had to step in or get help if a john got out of hand. Lotta Thyme and Barb Dwyer were working the Strathcona Hotel, the preferred watering hole for the city's young professionals and sports bar aficionados. The escort service included gals who worked the lucrative born-again Christian fundamentalist trade, choosing names like Joy Tudawerlde and Belle Ringer.

Luke Howard Fitzhugh, attending a weekend convention

of costume designers at the Dominion, stepped out of the lounge and crossed the lobby floor. As he viewed himself as a gentleman of distinction, he decided that he was only partially inebriated. If he'd been of the lower classes, he might have used the term half-swacked. In either case, he was certainly not blotto by any means, but he had to admit that his current condition rendered him more susceptible to female charms. In other words, if it moved, he ogled it.

Luke joined the throng waiting for the small hotel's single elevator. Catching a whiff of an alluring scent, Luke turned suddenly, his elbow striking the right breast of the beautiful woman standing behind him. He apologized profusely.

"If your heart is as soft as your breast," he said gallantly, "then I'm sure I'll be readily forgiven."

The woman looked Luke in the eye and smiled sweetly as the group entered the elevator and it began its upward ascent. Standing on tiptoes, she whispered in a throaty voice in Luke's ear, "My name's Thistle. And if your dick's as hard as your elbow, I'm in room 304!"

Luke struggled to fix the room number in his mind as the elevator door closed behind Thistle's swaying derrière.

Once settled in his room, Luke weighed the pros and cons of pursuing the woman's bold invitation. She was certainly seductive, and with the help of the sexual aid he'd obtained from the States, Luke was confident that he'd be more than capable of performing sexually.

He opened the mini-bar and chose a shot of brandy. As he lay back on the bed sipping the libation and viewing his silver-haired reflection in the mirror opposite, Luke was aware his little adventure was likely to cost him some money. Thistle had been dressed like a businesswoman, but the extreme décolletage and her sexual assertiveness had given her away. Well, nothing ventured, nothing gained. He reached for the phone and dialed room 304.

"This is Dusty," a sultry voice answered. "What can I do for you?"

"I'd like to speak with Thistle, please," Luke replied.
Thistle came on the line.

"We just met on the elevator," Luke reminded her. "I'd very much like to continue the conversation we were having."

"That would be naughty but nice," said Thistle, "which I want you to understand is the name of our company."

"Yes, I understand perfectly. How about coming up to my room for a drink?"

"That will be to our mutual pleasure, I'm sure. What's the number?"

"Five-four-six."

"Be up there shortly, honey," Thistle said, and hung up.

"Another sucker just took the bait," Thistle said to Dusty, who was sitting on the bench at her makeup table, wearing a lime green kimono with a black dragon across the back. "Have you got a date, too?"

Dusty took a deep drag on her cigarette, rested it on the ashtray in order to finish putting on her face and replied, "Guy I met in the bar. Pudgy but well-dressed. He's hell bent to get into my pants. People forget that ugly guys have to get laid, too."

Thistle turned to her own preparations, leaning into the bathroom mirror to check her appearance. Her eyes were a dark green, her pale golden skin in sharp contrast to her silky auburn hair. She swept her lashes with mascara, then blotted her freshly applied lipstick with a tissue. She stepped back into the bedroom, where she packed her carry bag with an assortment of creams, lotions and sexual toys, guaranteed to fulfill just about any erotic fantasy.

Thistle was a headstrong young woman with a troubled childhood. Her mother had died when she was seven, leaving her in the care of a father overly addicted to drink. The well-meaning minions at child welfare soon stepped in and shipped her off to be brought up by a stern aunt who'd lectured her on the dangers of heavy petting and, God forbid, sexual intercourse. Anything that ugly Aunt Olga declared taboo had only whetted young Thistle's curiosity, and she'd spent her teenage years building an impressive list of lovers eager to further her sexual education.

One admirer, a wealthy geek in her science class, desperately wanted to have sex with her, even though she was dating someone else. He offered her a hundred dollars to sleep with him. She flatly refused.

Wally persisted. "I'll be real fast. I'll throw the money on the floor, you bend down and I'll finish by the time you've picked it up."

Thistle replied, "I'll have to talk to my boyfriend first."

When she called him, the boyfriend said, "Ask him for $200 and pick up the money real fast. He won't even be able to get his pants down."

Thiustle accepted Wally's proposal. Over half an hour went by and the boyfriend was still waiting for her call. Finally, after forty-five minutes, he called her and asked, "What happened?"

Still breathing hard, Thistle managed to reply, "The bastard had all quarters."

In the process of getting a degree in social studies at the University of Victoria, Thistle ran up forty-five thousand dollars of student debt, including interest, which hung around her neck like an albatross.

She remembered reading about Carol Doda, a California college-student-cum-waitress. Carol had made a big name for herself, together with a lot of long green, by performing a bottoms only, all tits and teeth love act at the famous North Beach Condor Club in San Francisco, the first topless bar in the USA. Carol's charms had included a set of surgically enhanced, silicone injected hoochie coochies, and a classy chassis that drew national attention.

Her most famous dance was the topless and waterless swim. Doda did the Australian crawl, the Twist, the Frog and the Watusi, while the guys in the audience panted for a chance to do the breast stroke.

Thistle calmly assessed her own assets and determined a course of action as follows: *My set of Mary Poppins aren't too shabby, but they're just hanging around doing nothing. I've supported them in a 40D cup long enough. It's time they earned their keep.* She met Dusty Rhodes and Joy Tudawerlde, and together they launched an escort service. She paid off her student loan and at first, put quite a few bucks away. But the easy money soon had her hooked on expanding her wardrobe and acquiring the latest technological gadgets, so her bank balance fluctuated like a boom-and-bust economy. Her plans to get out of the business were postponed indefinitely.

Her client swung open his door at her discreet knock.

"Come in, my dear," he said. "Please make yourself comfortable. I took the liberty of ordering some champagne. It arrived just before you did. Will you join me in a glass or two of bubbly?"

"Of course," Thistle replied as she pressed up close to him. "How better to discuss our mutual admiration? I don't sleep with strangers, however. What did you say your name was, honey?"

"Luke. Luke Fitzhugh," he replied, not seeing any reason to conceal his identity. He put his arms around her, but Thistle broke away, saying, "Drinks and business first."

Luke went to the champagne bucket on the writing desk, popped the cork from a bottle, poured and handed a full glass to Thistle, who was showing a great deal of leg in one of the easy chairs.

"I don't come cheap," she declared. "How long do you want me to stay?"

"I have this problem," Luke said. "It will take a short time to ascertain if it's fixed." He launched into a brief explanation of his medical condition. "I suggest we run a tab to see if the bald-headed hermit will come out of his cave."

"Sounds fair enough, but I'm sure I can help you. The price range is $200 for a quickie, up to $750 for the whole night."

"You're on," Luke said eagerly.

"No, you first," Thistle insisted.

Luke peeled off several bills and handed them to Thistle. "This will start the tab," Luke said.

He held up a small bottle. "Aphrodisiac – a male version of Spanish fly in liquid form. It's supposed to increase sexual performance. I've already got the desire, now let's see if I can get my cherry splitter to work. Care to try some?"

"Mine's already split. Don't need it."

Luke looked at the bottle and read, "Fifteen drops in any drink. I'd better double the dose," he said, grinning lasciviously. "In for a nickel, in for a dime."

"I've heard of the stuff, but I've never come across it before. Are you sure you know what you're doing?"

Luke nodded, then quaffed the champagne quickly. They waited for the potion to kick in.

"You know, I had access to a crystal ball once," Luke said. "I rubbed it and a genie appeared. It gave me a choice between two things."

"Which were?" asked Thistle.

"I could either have a terrific memory or a long dick."

"And your choice was?"

"I can't remember," Luke deadpanned.

"Well, this I've got to see," said Thistle, laughing and holding up her glass for another drink. "Let me know when that stuff starts to work."

"Soon, I hope. I have to tell you, it was discouraging to recently find myself caught between panic and frustration."

"I don't follow you."

"Frustration is the first time you discover you can't do it the second time. And panic is the second time you discover you can't do it the first time!"

But then Luke felt his blood start to surge and swirl through his vital parts, and he drew Thistle to her feet. She placed her glass on a side table and pushed Luke down into the chair. Backing off, she began to remove her suit jacket and skirt, then her scarlet camisole and panties, until she stood naked before him.

Bug-eyed with lust, Luke jumped to his feet and began ripping off his own clothes. Thistle lay down on the bed and placed a pillow under her lovely posterior. Luke advanced on her with a highly engorged erection, a bonafide boner. He got as far as the foot of the bed when his eyes rolled back into his skull and he fell forward, uttering gurgling grunts.

Thistle rolled to one side, a low scream on her lips, as Luke collapsed face down onto the bed. Luke Howard Fitzhugh, costume designer, died happy with a hard-on. He'd been earnestly pursuing pleasure, but had had the misfortune to overtake it.

The situation was without precedent in Thistle's limited experience. What to do? Her mind struggled with the problem. *I didn't kill him. But are they going to believe me? Can they prove I was even here? Maybe.*

At first she had no idea who to turn to, but then it hit her: the go-to guy was her lawyer, Philip Figgwiggin. He'd extricated Thistle and the other girls from a common bawdyhouse rap a while back, then helped them form their company, even coming up with the name Naughty But Nice, Inc.

Thistle retrieved Figgwiggin's business card from her wallet and dialed his office. *Closed, damn it.* She called his residence and let the phone ring and ring.

Phil was heading out the door, on his way to a much-needed Gulf Islands holiday. He set his suitcase down and peered into the hallway mirror. He saw a tall, stoop-shouldered, trimly built man in his mid-fifties. His curly hair bore a few strands of gray, as did his neatly clipped moustache and goatee. There was a lively twinkle in his alert blue eyes.

He inspected his outfit, a tailored sports jacket and open-necked cotton shirt over L.L. Bean khakis, and adjudged himself presentable in the event that any romantic opportunities arose while he was away.

"Ever the optimist," he remarked aloud to his reflection.

Phil picked up his bag and was reaching for the door when he heard the phone. He took another step forward, but then something innate in his nature forced him to drop his suitbase and answer the persistent ringing. "What the hell does somebody want now?" he groused as he snatched up the receiver.

"Mr. Figgwiggin. Phil. I'm in deep trouble. I don't know what to do. Help me!"

Responding to the desperation in the somewhat familiar voice, Phil asked gently, "Who is this and what's the matter?"

"It's Thistle Fielgud. You know, from Naughty But Nice, Inc. And I've got a big problem down here at the Dominion Hotel."

"What kind of problem?"

"A guy dropped dead on me in his room!"

"I remember you now," said Figgwiggin, still trying to calm the caller. "I'm surprised it hasn't happened before this."

"Don't crack wise, Mr. Figgwiggin, this is serious."

"Okay, give me the basic details."

"Well, we were drinking, he took some stuff, something like Spanish fly, I think. We were just about to get it on when he dropped dead. Looks like a heart attack."

"Where are you now?"

"I'm standing naked in his hotel room looking at his body. What the hell should I do?"

Phil thought quickly. "I've got to know this, Thistle. Have you done anything culpable, I mean anything that you think might make you responsible for his death?"

"No!"

"Are you sure? Cross your heart."

"I'm sure."

"I can't advise you to lie, so it's up to you what you do. You can get dressed and ask the management to come up and deal with the situation, or you can operate on the principle that if at first you don't succeed, destroy all evidence that you tried. Are your fingerprints all over the room?"

"No. About all I had time to touch was the champagne glass I was drinking from."

"Were you smoking?"

"No."

"And you're calling from his phone?"

"No, my new cell phone."

"Your new what? Oh, never mind, I think I've heard of those. Okay, listen carefully, I'm going to tell you this only once. Your second option is more pragmatic. You could do this, but remember, I'm not saying you should. Wipe the champagne glass clean of your prints. Get dressed and pack up all your gear. Go out into the hall and start knocking on the door. If possible, have some guest see you doing that. Speak to them as they pass, and then, if you can, make a note of which room they go to. Then go to your own room, phone the front desk and tell them you're trying to reach what's-his-name. By the way, what *is* his name?"

"Luke Howard Fitzhugh, or so he told me."

"Hmm, no one I know. Make sure you haven't left any traces on his clothes. Okay, tell the management you had a dinner engagement with Fitzhugh and he's not answering his phone or his door. Do they want to check his room to see if he's all right? Have you got all that?"

"Yes. When can I see you?"

"Not for a week, I'm afraid. I'm going on holiday. I can't do any more for you now, anyway. Either plan of action should work. I'm advising you to use the first one, but the second doesn't get you involved, if you're lucky."

Phil hung up the phone and left his condo, hoping he wasn't going to end up in another legal wrangle involving Canada's archaic prostitution laws. He mused that the fatal victims of prostitution were usually the prostitutes, not ' johns. In this case, one might say Fitzhugh had it com·

Doggerel Don McGraw

In every complex there lives some tenant with writing talent, some unsung Robert Service, some person born with an instinct for poverty, some would-be poet laureate no one will appreciate until he's dead. The Whynan Beach Road condo complex in Victoria's Fairfield district, where Phil Figgwiggin lived, was no exception; Doggerel Don McGraw lived in apartment seventeen.

Another commodity not in short supply was the risqué joke. Don believed these jokes contained nuggets of wisdom and that it was a mistake to dismiss them summarily. His particular talent was the ability to take any so-called dirty joke and turn it into a poem.

That very morning he had heard a good one in the Y Knot coffee shop at the downtown YM-YWCA, and had been mentally composing a draft. Now he decided to commit it to paper:

A man standing at the corner saw a blind man with a seeing-eye dog.

As they approached, the signal changed and the dog made the two of them stop

He saw that the dog raised his leg up, the observer was all agog

He watched as it peed on the blind man's foot, he clearly needed a mop.

The blind man didn't do as expected, like soundly rebuking the hound.

Instead, he reached into his pocket and took a dog treat from there.

By now the observer had reached them, and to them he made his first sound

"I wouldn't think you'd reward him, if you do, you are a strange pair."

"Far from it," the blind man retorted. "Necessity means that I must

"First find out where his head is, that's why with my hand I pass

"The biscuit in front of his nostrils, and I sincerely hope and I trust

"To put the right end in front of me and give him a boot in the ass!"

Don, ever in need of audience approval, took his latest opus to Phil Figgwiggin. He caught up with the lawyer in the elevator.

Phil was heading down to the basement garage to pick up his car. He was worried he'd miss his ferry, so when Don opportuned him, Phil was courteous enough, but his expression made it clear he wasn't happy to see the scrawny doggerel monger. "What can I do for you, Don?"

"I want you to read this," Don replied, thrusting the poem into Phil's hand. Accustomed to perusing lengthy documents at speed, Phil gave it a cursory look. "I can tell it's poetry," he commented. "Do you know how I can tell?'

"How?" asked Don, hoping the answer would acknowledge his talent and be complimentary to boot.

"Every line starts with a capital letter," Phil replied, deadpan. "What do you call this literary masterpiece?"

"Necessity is the Mother of Invention," Don replied. "What do you think?"

"I've already heard the joke, and the poetry stinks."

Not exactly the praise Don had been seeking, but you can't win 'em all, he consoled himself. *It'd be nice to win some, though.* "Thanks a bunch, Phil. You sure know how to hurt a guy."

As he returned to his own digs, Don muttered, "Why did I bother asking his opinion?"

Never mind, he had greater aspirations. He was writing a book entitled Homosaurus Rex, about a morbidly obese guy confined to a hospital fat ward. The protagonist's dream was to stay in one of a chain of California resorts called Orca Flats, where people who were too fat to walk spent their days in the water like walruses. At night they slept in float homes in a marina.

When Rex arrives at Orca Flats he finds the operators intend to use him in cloning experiments with gray whales, to create a hybrid creature that could survive the next great flood, live on wet star satellites and perform slave labour for the satellite's overlords.

Rex thinks he's escaped this fate until they try to mate him with a huge Nigerian who tells him she was kidnapped as part of a diabolical plot run by the CIA. The plot is thwarted by a six-thousand-pound mermaid with breasts the size of Ethel Merman's and a brain the size of Albert Einstein's. Rex falls for the mermaid hook, line and sinker, providing the romantic interest for the novel.

Back in his apartment, Don turned on the radio in the faint hope of hearing some good news for a change. Most of the time, the news was too true to be good. He stopped twisting the dial when he heard a DJ laugh as he announced: *This bit that I'm going to play next was sent in by a listener.* He continued in the gravelly voice of a racetrack announcer:

Welcome to the third race at the Honeymoon is Over Downs. They're at the gate and they're OFF! Jumping out in the lead is

Romance and Affection with Domestic Bliss close behind. It's Romance and Affection and Domestic Bliss.

Here comes Marriage Vows followed by Immediate Child. Romance and Affection is falling off quickly. Mortgaged Up the Ass is overtaking Domestic Bliss. And here comes Nasty Attitude followed by More Children and Drinking Heavily.

Coming down the backstretch, it's Drinking Heavily moving out in front of Mortgaged up the Ass. But coming up strong on the outside is Credit in Shambles. It's Credit in Shambles, followed by I Don't Give a Shit, Nasty Attitude and Up Yours.

Up Yours is challenging for second going into the clubhouse turn. Passing on the rail is I Don't Give a Shit, who takes the lead, followed by Keep the Fucking House, You Cook Like Shit, and I Fucked Your Brother.

Here they come spinning out of the turn. I Don't Give a Shit is still in front. Up Yours is challenging for the lead. Up Yours and I Don't Give a Shit are neck and neck.

And down the stretch they come. Up Yours is pulling away from I Don't Give a Shit. Up Yours is in front by a length, followed by I Don't Give a Shit, and passing the pack is Keep the Fucking House. Coming on strong is I Am Out of Here.

At the wire it's Up Yours, Keep the Fucking House, I Don't Give a Shit and I am Out of Here!

Doggerel Don wished he could write like that. He considered a number of names for racehorses, such as Ménage A Trois, Kinky Lingerie, or Cunning Stunt. Perhaps what his poetry lacked was refinement, a bit of the classical touch, or maybe the Dan Brown treatment. He sat down at his dining room table, waiting for inspiration. What should he call his next opus? Then the title came to him: No Wonder Mona Smiled. He again put pencil to paper:

This is the sad story of a Frenchman, a cat burglar who knocked over the Louvre.

He was already a well-known art thief, but felt he had something to prove.

On pussycat feet he avoided alarms and went straight to the master's art,

He skipped the obscure and went for the best and soon began loading his cart.

Leonardo DaVinci's Mona Lisa was one that he fancied a lot,

And a Rubens, a Titian, a Rembrandt he decided to take on the spot.

He put them all in his satchel and safely returned to the street,

And he jumped in his van and departed at the sound of approaching feet.

But this is the point where his luck runs out, the vehicle sputters and stops,

It takes no more than a minute for the place to be swarming with cops.

If only he could have kept going, the stop was a terrible blow,

For he had no Monet to buy Degas to make the old Van Gogh!

Whynan Beach Road

Phil Figgwiggin's neighbors were a mixed bag indeed. Sal Vachon, an itinerant preacher for twenty years, lived in the not-so-grand penthouse of the Whynan Beach Road condo complex with his equally religious significant other, Starr Vachon. The couple loved their lofty perch in the highrise and seized every chance to lord it over the unwashed pagan peasantry in the apartments below.

Sal filled in for ministers of the Seventh Day Absentist Church, when those other men of God became ill or were on vacation. His sermons were like water to a drowning man, but at the end of each and every one there was a tremendous awakening.

The Vachons were empty nesters and, like most families, had had their share of trials and tribulation. Starr had borne two children: a girl, Elizabeth, whom everyone called Ellie, and a boy who was a midget. At school the kids called him young Master Vachon. He turned out to be a gay midget and eventually came out of the cupboard.

With both kids now gone, Sal and Starr were alone on this sunny Saturday morning during which, unbeknownst to them, a fowl fiasco of religious complexity was brewing.

They were in violation of one clause in the strata agreement that theoretically controlled the development, namely the regulation stipulating no pets.

The penthouse sported a small rooftop patio, complete with a small artificial pond surrounded by plant life – an oasis open to the summer sky and the nearby waterfront, where seagulls screeched as they fought over handouts from strolling tourists.

Sal had a fowl passion: he had always loved chickens. He kept three of them, each of some exotic variety, in a cage on the patio. Unable to fly, the chickens had the run of the apartment and the roof garden. Sal had named them Foghorn Leghorn, Cacciatore and Kentucky Fried.

At first Starr had objected to his hobby. "Think of the smell," she said, wrinkling her bulbous nose.

"Don't worry, they'll soon get used to it," Sal replied.

Many denizens of the complex were less than enthusiastic about their religious neighbors and their penthouse pets.

Harvey Lode, an emotionally depressed trucker who worked for the Saanichsaurus Wrecks auto scrapyard once quipped to Phil, "I hear he's holy unemployed."

"I've heard his sermons; he gets a kneeling ovation from his congregation every week," was Phil's reply.

"You've gotta watch him," Harvey chimed in again. "He'll try to convert you. He caught me in the elevator last week and tried to explain the Trinity theory of the Father, the Son and the Holy Ghost."

"You mean Big Daddy, Junior and the Spook?"

Meanwhile, up in the penthouse, Sal and Starr Vachon heard a commotion out on the patio – chickens screeching and clucking, then silence.

"Likely some seagull trying to screw one of the chickens again," said Starr, going back to her lunch preparations.

"That reminds me of the parable of the Three Bears," said Sal from his position in the living room's recliner. "One of them screwed a giraffe. The other two put him up to it." He continued reading his paper, but after ten minutes, decided he'd better go investigate. He rose and sauntered through the sliding glass doors out onto the roof.

He looked around and at first saw nothing amiss. Two of his prize chickens were in the wire cage. But where was Kentucky Fried, the third chicken?

"Oh, my God!" Sal cried, as he spotted the bird floating feet up in the pond, her head pointing straight at the bottom of the pool.

Sal snatched Kentucky from what he hoped was not a watery grave. The bird lay apparently lifeless in his hands. Sal was frantic. *How did this happen? I must save her!*

He began to squeeze the bird's chest in an attempt to force air into its lungs. Nothing. He shook the bird in desperation. Still no response.

So Sal started to pray: "Oh Lord, Thou who art a brother to jackals and a companion to apes and ostriches, give this bird hope, for a living chicken is better than a dead lion. Let this Kentucky Fried Chicken flutter again over her young and make this fowl of heaven run once more."

God apparently wasn't buying Sal's pleas. Kentucky was, to all intents and purposes, kaput.

Sal, saddened but with pressing business elsewhere, had to cease and desist in his efforts to revive his pet, and left her in the care of his wife. Starr was nonplussed, but decided to call her good friend, Beth Tubbe, a massage therapist and nurse, who might know what to do.

Beth came over to the apartment, primarily for coffee and cakes, but took a look at the exotic bird lying inert on the coffee table. The first remedy that occurred to her was to thoroughly dry the bird's feathers and apply heat. No luck.

"Nothing else for it," Beth said. "Gotta try mouth-to-beak resuscitation." She pried open the bird's beak and began to puff air into it. After several applications of the breath of life, Starr let out a yell. "Lord love a duck! Its eyes opened!"

Sure enough they had, and after a further session, Kentucky's head moved. Just then Sal returned.

"I'd thought of the Heinlikker maneuver," he said on learning what had happened, "but didn't think of – well, let me give it a try."

Sal liked chickens a lot, but he'd never gone so far as to kiss one. Now he did, cradling Kentucky in his arms and giving her mouth-to-beak. After all, she *was* female. The bird again opened its eyes and moved its head, but that was all.

"Let's give it a rest and try again later," Sal suggested. They wrapped the bird in a towel and put her in a shoebox in a warm corner of the condo. Beth left at that point.

Starr sat nearby, picked up her illustrated Bible and began to read. She loved the pictures and always read a chapter each day, trying to more fully understand its many lessons. Some things she didn't understand at all, such as why everyone at the Last Supper sat on the same side of the table.

She came to John 11:43-44, which described how Lazarus was raised from the dead. Starr read aloud: "*Now a certain man was ill, Lazarus of Bethany, in the village of Mary and her sister Martha. And they sent for Jesus, and Martha said to him, Lord, if you had been here, my brother would not have died. And even now I know that whatever you ask God, God will give you. Jesus said to her, Your brother Lazarus will rise again.*"

Suddenly the shoebox began to shake wildly as Starr read on: "*Jesus said with a loud voice, Lazarus, come out. The dead man came out–*"

The lid of the shoebox flew off and Kentucky Fried staggered out of her cardboard coffin. She let out a loud squawk and began to stumble around the room.

Starr let out a surprised shriek and yelled out Sal's name. "Come here, quick!" she screamed.

Sal came running into the living room. "It's a miracle!" he exclaimed. "Kentucky Fried is not dead, but has come home and is gathered unto the children of God who are scattered abroad. It is for the glory of God, so that the Son of God may be glorified by means of it. Thank you, Jesus. This shall prove to the heathens that there is a God. I've saved the pheasantry, I must now proselytize the peasantry!"

Hornby Island

One of Phil's colleagues had put him onto Hornby Island when Phil mentioned he was looking for a quiet getaway. The other lawyer was a child when he and his family first stayed at Seabreeze Guest Farm, and now he took his own kids there every summer. Open for most of the year, the peak season was the summer holidays, but with unseasonably warm weather, many people made the trek in May. When Phil called to book a room, the owner had asked, "So, how would you like your mollies coddled?"

"Say again?"

"Any food allergies? Special requests?"

"No lawyer jokes."

Phil headed north over the Malahat, up-Island toward Nanaimo, where he caught a ferry to Denman Island, then on the opposite side of Denman, drove onto the six-car ferry for the last leg of his trip to Hornby.

Coming off the ferry, Phil observed that the sea between the two islands was indeed turquoise, as promised by his colleague. The shore road toward Seabreeze gave him frequent glimpses of sandstone cliffs and crashing surf. When he pulled into the yard at the guest farm, there was a man front porch of the main house, blasting away on a trombone. Spotting the car, the musician put down his instrument, descended the steps and waved Phil to a parking space around the back.

As Phil got out, the man stepped forward and offered his hand, saying, "Welcome. I'm Mike Fowler. My wife Evelyn and I run this place."

"Phil Figgwiggin. I understand from my friend that you've owned Seabreeze for quite some time."

"Thirty-two years. You shoulda seen it in the early days. I wanted to call it Callused Palms." Walking Phil toward the house, Mike asked, "And how're ya feelin' this bonny day?"

"If I felt any better, I'd throw up."

Phil always made a point of coming up with a new answer to the oft-asked question, figuring people really didn't give a rat's ass how you felt. If they said, "How're you doin'?" he might reply, "Everybody I can and the suckers twice."

"You're just in time for lunch," Mike said. "Follow me to the dining room. We'll get you settled in a cabin later."

"You're pretty good on the trombone," Phil remarked as they entered the building.

"Nah, the trombone's an ill wind that nobody blows good. The bass fiddle's more my thing," said Mike.

"And what was that tune you were playing?"

"It's the butcher's song, We'll Meat Again."

Phil chuckled, then asked, "Do you know the ass is hanging out of your pants?"

"No, but hum a few bars and I may get it," Mike replied without missing a beat, then added, "Meat's what we're having for lunch. Along with a Caesar salad, and some of my wife's strawbapple pie with a choice of cheese for afters. I guarantee you won't throw that lot up."

The meal, shared at a huge country kitchen table with eleven other guests, was better than advertised, thanks to the culinary skills of Evelyn Fowler. She made numerous trips to and from the kitchen, serving up the food with a smile and a cheerful word for each guest. Several times as she passed

Mike, he grabbed her and pulled her into an embrace, pretending to leer. Evelyn just giggled and leaned in closer. One of the others told Phil the couple had been married for more than thirty-five years, and Phil found himself enjoying the Fowlers' easy banter and obvious love for each other.

After lunch, Evelyn escorted Phil to one of the older wood-shingled cabins, its front door shaded by an awning over the porch. "It has the best view," she explained. Phil, enchanted by the cliffside location and the wide beach that stretched several hundred yards in either direction, heartily agreed and thanked his hostess, who left him to unpack.

Phil spied a young family frolicking in the surf, the children's shrieks barely audible. He took in the room's décor which, complete with an old-fashioned radio, bespoke an earlier era. The stone floor was generously covered with thick rugs. A brightly coloured throw served as a bedcover, and an overstuffed armchair flanked the bed. A small television sat in the opposite corner. An alcove, a recent addition, turned out to be a more contemporary three-piece bath, whose every surface gleamed.

Phil felt his whole body sigh in relief, and he surprised himself by sinking onto the bed for an afternoon nap.

He awoke to a sonorous metallic clanging, repeated at ten-second intervals. Glancing at the watch he'd laid on the bedside table, he was startled to realize the sound must be the dinner bell. He quickly freshened up and changed, threw on a jacket against the evening chill and made his way to the guesthouse.

There he saw Mike swing a mallet one last time as guests streamed past him heading into the house.

"That's original," said Phil, pointing at the makeshift gong hanging over the porch.

"Empty WWII shell casing," Mike replied with a grin. "Fired at the Japanese by a Canadian ship. Not military, though."

"Interesting. How did you come by it? Must be a story attached."

"Sure is. A guest called Ernest Holden gave it to me. He was the Chief Steward on a CPR Coastal Steamship, the *Princess Maquinna*, one of several ships that were armed with naval guns during World War Two. They were supposed to be used by crews trained for defence against enemy attack. Holden's ship fired its artillery piece at what, rightly or wrongly, they took to be a Japanese sub. Holden kept the shell casing in his personal possession until he gave it to me."

"That could have some historical significance," Phil remarked. "We may be looking at the only shell ever fired by a non-military steamship at the enemy in World War Two."

"And now it's my dinner bell," said Mike with pride.

"You should donate it to the Naval Museum in Victoria."

"Good idea. I'll keep that in mind for when I move there."

At supper, Phil sat next to a tall man in his early thirties. Phil noted the man's rugged good looks, wavy hair, well-trimmed moustache and steady brown eyes.

"Neale Downe's the name," Phil's companion said, offering his hand after loading his plate with roast beef and plenty of trimmings. "Friend of Mike's. I'm not a guest here, but I come by when I can for one of these great Fowler suppers."

"Phil Figgwiggin. Glad to meet you. This home cooking is excellent, I agree."

While the others at the table, two young couples with a trio of children each, traded childrearing tales, Phil and Neale chatted easily about Seabreeze and Gulf Islands life in general. Downe said he'd had a place on the island for six years and occasionally traveled to Victoria, but otherwise lived a semi-hermit life.

"City doesn't have much appeal for me anymore," was all he said when Phil expressed curiosity.

As he helped himself to a third portion of everything, Neale asked Phil, "What do you think about pot?"

"Say again?"

"Reefers, grass, cannabis, hemp."

"Why do you ask?" Phil replied, ever wary of getting into legal issues outside the office.

"I have good reason, which I may explain later."

Thinking that this would be as good a time as any to keep his mouth shut, Phil nevertheless couldn't help but answer, "I'm aware that millions of Canadians have tried marijuana. Its cultivation brings in billions of dollars in BC alone. I think we're in the midst of a clash between smokers, growers, police and politicians over how to handle it."

"Do you think it should be decriminalized?"

"Should we make it legal? Certainly."

"And why is that?"

"Well, if it were legal, not only would our prisons be emptier, the crop could be controlled and taxed, just like tobacco. And the government could oversee some sort of quality control system."

"Wouldn't be as expensive as it is now," Neale said, nodding eagerly. "Although the government would load on the taxes, all right."

Given his receptive audience, the orator in Phil warmed to his theme. "I feel it's time Ottawa ended its eighty-four-year-old prohibition against marijuana by regulating its production, distribution and consumption, the same as it does for alcohol. You asked, that's my opinion. Why are you interested?"

"I heard you were a lawyer, which is why I sat next to you. I may need one, but if so, I'd want to know his stand on pot. I was a grower and I got ripped off by the Mounties."

Phil's interest was piqued, but he replied, "This isn't my office and I'm on holiday."

"I understand," said Neale, nodding his thanks to Evelyn as he accepted an after-dinner coffee. "I'm just making conversation. I'm out of the business now, anyway."

"What do you mean, they ripped you off?"

"They were just doing their job, I guess, enforcing the anti-pot laws. All they got was the crop; they didn't get me.

But the Mounties don't come to Hornby all that often, so they must have been tipped off."

"Yes, but I'm sure you knew the score. You took that risk and it didn't pay off."

"But where does that leave me? I worked my ass off for nothing."

"As a matter of interest, how did they find the grow-op?"

"I had it on a nearly inaccessible steep slope. There was an old road above the slope and I ran a plastic hose from the edge of the road down to the crop. That's how I supplied the water – from a big tank on my truck. Some hiker must have seen the end of the hose, followed it down, found the site and reported it to the cops."

"That's too bad. So why would you need a lawyer now? I assume that earlier matter was resolved one way or the other, and since you're not in the racket anymore…"

Taking a deep breath, Neale replied, "I've been thinking over the whole pot problem and the way we handle it. Giving Canadians criminal records for personal behavior that's less harmful than tobacco or alcohol is just plain stupid. I'm just trying to keep some future ahead of me instead of dwelling on what's in the past. If I decide to go into a grow-op again and I get caught, I'd want to fight the issue in the courts. And that's when I'd need a good lawyer who was willing to go to bat for me."

At that point, Mike piped up from the other end of the table: "Okay, folks, it's showtime! If you've got musical talent, I want ya front and centre."

He led the way into the living room, where a fire burned in the grate and three sofas surrounded an upright piano and Mike's double bass.

Needing no urging, one of the young fathers slid onto the piano bench and warmed up with a few riffs. Mike stepped up to his bass, gave it a couple of twirls and launched into a bass run. The pianist picked up the motif and expanded on it with a lively improvisation, while his wife kept the beat on a series of mugs and glasses she'd set up on the coffee table.

Seeing toes tapping all around, Mike launched into his favourite comic song:

She's lazy and she's lousy and she loves it
She sleeps all day and at night she goes to bed
She keeps her bathtub full of beer
Smokes a pipe for atmosphere
Loves to hit her sister with a hammer on the head
She's satisfied to be the way she is
Because the way she is –
Is lazy, lousy and she loves it!

The mothers took their young kids off to bed, but the music and jokes carried on until much later in the evening. Mike sang some other ditties, such as I Used to Kiss Her on the Lips, But It's All Over Now; and one that included the lines, She was only a banker's daughter but you should have seen her face when the safe blew. "Can't resist this one, folks," Mike yelled as he rendered the next gem:

Mary went for a sleighride,
Landed in the snow upside down,
Mary lay there screamin'
M'ass is in the cold, cold ground.

Phil, knowing he needed to recharge, took his leave around ten-thirty. He cracked open the cabin's window and, aided by the pristine ocean breeze, tumbled into the deepest sleep he'd known in months.

The next morning he took the trail down to the beach, where he wandered among the strange outcroppings of rock left from some long-ago volcanic action. He explored the tide pools and generally spent the day releasing what little tension was left in him. Evelyn had sensed his need for time alone, so she'd packed him a generous picnic lunch complete with a thermos of hot coffee, so he could bask in the sunshine all day if he chose to.

Late in the afternoon, he found himself drifting toward the barn, where Mike had assembled the children for a demonstration of cow-milking technique. The kids eagerly jostled for a chance to take their turn, then ran off happily after much squealing and errant spraying while Mike cleaned up the mess.

"It never stops for you, does it?" Phil asked.

"Gotta keep the ankle-biters entertained," he replied. With a conspiratorial wink, he added, "Gives their parents time for their own fun. Don't know how much longer we'll be doing it, though."

Mike hoisted the two pails of milk and headed for the house. "Both Evelyn and I are getting tired. I'm 63, after all. Maybe it's time to slow down a little."

The next day, Mike decided to revive the summer tradition of the Hornby Island Hayride. With horses hitched to the wagon, Mike issued each person a P ticket, good for one pee stop when presented to the driver. Ticket holders had to mark their preferred stopping places – trees, bushes or the wheat field.

Phil wasn't about to miss out, so he clambered aboard and wedged himself between two boys, who giggled as they tossed hay back and forth, catching Phil in the crossfire. He grabbed one child and pretended to heave him over the side.

When the ride passed by the sign denoting the main competitor to Seabreeze, Mike got off, doffed his hat and spat on the sign, then invited his passengers to do likewise.

On the way back, he led a rousing chorus of Seabreeze for Me, which extolled the virtues of the Fowler establishment and poked fun at the opposition.

Late that evening Phil couldn't sleep, so he bundled up and wandered over to the guesthouse to find Mike already lounging on the verandah. "Insomnia, huh?" Mike asked.

"More and more often," Phil replied. "No point fighting it, I generally get up and find something productive to do." He dropped onto the two-seater sofa facing the water and watched the twinkling lights off Texada Island to the east.

Mike was the first to break the silence. "Well, if we're gonna sit here, we might as well get comfortable. Back in a jiff." He stepped inside and returned carrying a tray laden with a box of cigars, a bottle and two glasses.

Phil gratefully accepted a brandy, but declined the cigar. "I used to smoke, but quit. So how did you get into this business, Mike? Family history of hotel management, that sort of thing?"

"Nothing like that," Mike replied, biting off the end of his cigar and taking a moment to light it. "So ya want the life story, eh?" At Phil's nod of encouragement, he continued, "Like a mosquito in a nudist camp, I hardly know where to start. I've had so many jobs, I wouldn't know what kinda work I was out of.

"Back in the war I was in the merchant navy. Learned wire splicing, machining, diving and explosives. Lotta that came in handy in the oil patch later. I was a sideman in a few bands in the Fifties. Never hit it big, though I played with some names back in the day. I was married to Evelyn by then; fell for her like a blind roofer. Anyway, gigs finishing after midnight and that whole booze and pot scene, it just didn't fit with married life, so after a while I packed it in."

"Neale tells me you also play the bagpipes," Phil prompted.

"Yeah. They say a true gentleman knows how to play the pipes – but doesn't." Grinning at Phil, he added, "Guess we know what that makes me, eh? So what about you, Phil? Been lawyering all your working life?"

"That, and stand-up comedy to keep my sanity."

"Well, good on ya," Mike exclaimed. "Ya gotta keep laughing, I say. There's enough sour faces around, and I never wanna be one of them."

Phil seconded that, then reached for the brandy bottle. After topping up their glasses, the two men leaned back, content to let the night birds and the soft slap of ocean waves provide the conversation.

Two Propositions

Even though he recognized that half the people he knew were below average, Don McGraw was tired of living alone and seriously considering getting married. He thought of contacting Bachelors Anonymous. If you called them, they sent a woman around in the early morning, wearing curlers, and she nagged you for half an hour.

McGraw ran over the pros and cons in his mind. Could he stand the aggravation? He'd have to learn to work the toilet seat unless he wanted to hear a lot of bitching. He'd have to know what day it was and remember birthdays and anniversaries, then pick out perfect presents for each one.

I don't know the answers to every question, and I don't like answering questions I don't want to hear. I don't like foreign films. On the other hand I have different fingers. I'm lonely, my testosterone is raging and I'd really appreciate some feminine companionship.

At the moment however, Don had some business to attend to down at Gaston Ready's condo in the same complex. He was also eager to see Gaston's girlfriend Ann Kerzaway. She was a looker, pleasantly plump with curves in all the right places, and he enjoyed simply gazing at her.

Ann and Gaston lived in condo 206, but they hadn't been together long enough for the arrangement to constitute a common-law relationship. She had lost her maidenhead but not her maiden name, which was virgo intacto, unsullied by marriage vows. Ann had to admit that it would be nice to get a surname less subject to facetious remarks. But she was having second thoughts about her live-in lover.

Gaston's true loves were the martial arts and stock car racing. Ann had met Gas in his manic stage when everything was fun, but she had come to learn that depression, the opposite pole of his condition, was merely anger without enthusiasm.

Gas held down a regular job as a doughnut salesman at Tim Hortons, but Ann suspected that was only a cover for whatever it was he really did. She knew he was making fairly big money on the side, although he sure hadn't been spending it on her, and that was starting to bug her.

Gaston was in the shower and Ann was brushing her teeth in the adjacent bathroom, wearing only a dressing gown and a smile, when the doorbell rang.

"You'll have to get that," Gaston yelled from behind the curtain.

Ann opened the door with her toothbrush still in her mouth, to see that their visitor was their cliff-dwelling neighbour Doggerel Don McGraw.

Athough this hadn't been the purpose of his visit, Don blurted, "I'll give you eight hundred dollars if you drop that dressing gown." He pulled a wad of bills out of his pocket.

Ann was taken aback, but after considering the offer for a few seconds, she let her dressing gown fall to the floor and allowed Don a good long look. She was suddenly conscious of having put on a few pounds, but she was gratified to see the half-tender, half-lascivious look on Don's face as he handed her the bills and left.

Ann stuck the money in a pocket of the dressing gown and went back into the bathroom.

"Who was it?" Gas asked brusquely as he toweled off.

"Just Don McGraw. Dropped in to say hello, but left 'cause we're busy."

"He say anything about the $800 he owes me?"

Ann nearly jabbed out one of her tonsils with the toothbrush, but she kept her cool. She made a show of spitting and rinsing as she thought. *I could say yes, but I want to keep this little bonanza. I could say no and it would teach that Don a big lesson. He'll say he paid the debt, but it would be his word against mine. If he tells Gaston he paid for a peek, will Gas believe him?*

"No," she finally said, patting her mouth dry with a hand towel.

Back in his own apartment, Don contemplated one other reason he'd wanted to visit Ann and Gaston. As usual, he'd hoped to show off his latest poem. He was proud of this one, as it was written like a classified ad.

Gorilla My Dreams
WANTED: Male Volunteer for
Research Project
$500 – Call for Details

This was the ad the newspaper had in its classified
And this also was the very one our subject had espied
He was a Newfoundlander a bit down on his luck
So he called for an appointment, it took a bit of pluck.
They said to come tomorrow, he showed up on the dot
He wasn't going to miss a trick; he was Johnny on the spot
A white-lab-coated scientist then took him by the hand
"We want to tell you of the project, and the thing that we have planned.
"What we want to know, would a gorilla female mate
"With a human male partner, we'd like to contemplate
"Just what would be the outcome? And that's where you come in.

"To have sex with the gorilla, it's for science, it's not sin."

The Newfie thought it over. "Well, for science I'll consent

"But first there are conditions to this experiment,

"I will not kiss her on the lips, I won't do that at all

"To have gorilla lips upon mine really does appall.

"I will not stay the whole night, is condition number two

"As soon as we have finished, I'm out of here, I'm through.

"And finally the third one, we come to number three

"Though I really wish this whole affair could be condition free.

"It's all about the money; you said five hundred bucks?

"I do not want to pull out now, and though I know it sucks

"You'll have to take instalments, there is no other way,

"But if you'll only trust me, I'm sure that I can pay."

Still worried about the episode with Don, Ann decided to take the offensive. "You know what, Gas? You've forgotten something and it really is cheesing me off."

"Oh yeah? And what's that?"

"The anniversary of our first date. How could you forget that? The time you told me I was the girl of your dreams."

"You were, but I woke up."

"Very funny."

"I gotta get outa here. Gotta meet somebody on Hornby Island. I won't be home for a few days."

"Why are you going up to Hornby?"

"To see a man about a dog. Just never mind."

"You're using the car again while I have to walk. So listen carefully, I'm only gonna tell you this once. If I don't see some kinda present around here soon – something that goes from zero to 140 in 10 seconds, you can take a flying fuck at a rubber duck, you insensitive SOB."

Betty Crocker Rides Again

On Phil's last evening at Seabreeze, Mike approached him as he sat on the verandah drinking coffee with Neale Downe.

"Did you bring any brownies, Neale?" Mike asked.

"Matter of fact, I did."

"Then I say we invite Phil here down to the old beach house later. I'll ask Doc Dickout to come along, too."

"Damn good idea," Neale exclaimed.

Turning to Phil, Mike added, "The doc's the one with the three red-headed kids."

Phil, wondering whether this was some kind of set-up, observed Mike. The innkeeper was still in good shape, not yet at the stage where everything hurts and what doesn't hurt doesn't work. To Phil it seemed Mike was still up for whatever fun and games were to be had.

"Why not?" Phil said aloud. "The night is young and none of you are beautiful."

"Okay, see you guys down there in a bit. Bring a jacket; it cools off fast by the beach."

The beach house was old and decrepit. The others were already sitting around inside by the time Phil arrived, and

Mike had a cheery fire crackling away in the iron cook stove.

"Looks like the old hot stove league," said Phil, as he made himself comfortable on the floor. "As a kid on the Prairies, I used to go the village general store. The same group of local farmers would sit around a red-hot potbellied stove telling stories, talking crops and listening to the sizzle as they spat on the stove."

"Bet they never had anything like this, though," Mike said with a chuckle as he passed around a plate of brownies, then took one himself.

"And these are. . .?" Phil asked out courtesy, although he figured he knew.

"Since smoking is falling so far into disrepute, this is the best way to ingest some very excellent cannabis," said Neale. "The famous and very yummy Hornby Island Time Warp grass."

"Hmm," Phil answered, selecting one of the squares and contemplating it. "I suppose this way when they ask you if you've smoked pot, you can honestly say you haven't."

"I have a deal with Neale," said Mike. "This stuff makes for a change and fixes a problem I'm having with beer. Gotta talk to you about that, Doc. I think I'm allergic to beer."

"What are your symptoms?" the young physician asked.

"Every time I drink ten or twelve beers I throw up."

The men laughed and exchanged glances as they felt the euphoric effects of the weedy brownies kick in.

"So Doc, as a medical man, what's your take on hemp?" Mike wanted to know.

"It's a magnificent plant, known as a healing agent for thousands of years, and one of the safest remedies around." Dickout bit into a brownie, masticated slowly, swallowed, then said, "It's effective for a range of conditions, including asthma, emphysema, glaucoma, tumors, nausea, cancer, seasickness, epilepsy, back pain, muscle spasms, arthritis, herpes, cystic fibrosis and rheumatism.

"A great expectorant, too. Cleans up the lungs. It can help you sleep or just relax, it relieves stress and migraines, and it's an appetite stimulant. It's safer than Valium, Librium or alcohol. Smokers should switch to cannabis – although that wouldn't be good news for the tobacco companies.

"Long lecture, I guess, but it's an insult to the medical profession that we can't use marijuana as a healing tool, and that the police, politicians and prosecutors can stop people from having recourse to this kind of natural therapy."

"If you'd gone on any longer, I'd have set up a podium," Mike quipped.

He added more wood to the fire, then said thoughtfully, "I'm older than you guys and I can remember as a kid in the States – this was back before 1937 – when hemp was a legal crop. Smoking pot for relaxation was only one small use, because the main one was in the paper industry. In about 1916, they invented some kind of hemp harvesting machinery. They also used hemp to manufacture explosives and munitions. As far as paper-producing capacity, hemp out-performed forest products four to one, and you could renew the hemp crop every few months."

"That being so, why was it outlawed?" Phil asked.

"Follow the money, as usual. The Hearst Manufacturing Division owned a shitload of timberland, and the DuPonts had just patented a process to make plastic from coal and oil. These rich corporate guys used their newspapers to rant against hemp paper and natural plastic technology. They had outfits like the Mellon Bank in Pittsburgh behind them. All these guys knew they'd lose billions of dollars if hemp crops took over from timber and oil."

"So what did they do?" asked Neale.

"Mellon was Herbert Hoover's treasury secretary in 1931. He set up the Federal Bureau of Narcotics and Dangerous Drugs, then imposed a transfer tax of two hundred bucks – that'd be eight or ten thousand bucks today – on hemp growers. They wanted to drive the small producers

out of business. In 1937, they declared marijuana a dangerous drug and made it illegal to grow it. You all know the
result: the ultra-stupid War on Drugs we have today."

Into the ensuing silence, Neale said, "What bugs me is
that everyone with any brains knows these laws are insane,
that the so-called War on Drugs is a complete failure and
that cannabis isn't harmful. Yet they don't do a damn thing
about it."

"We all realize the difference between hemp per se and
the pot we've just eaten," said Phil.

"Sure we do," Mike said. "And I'm also sure Neale could
explain the whole process of how you get from hemp to the
narcotic."

Neale began, "The THC we just ate –"

"Delta-9-tetrohydrocannabinol," said the doctor. "The
hallucinogenic element."

"Yeah, that you get from the buds of the female cannabis
plant only, which have to be kept separate from the male.
These are processed and you get pot. That's about all you
need to know."

"You're so right there," said Mike. "We're getting a little
too serious here, fellas." Helping himself to another brownie, he added, "These little guys remind me of a lumberjack
who comes home from a stint in the woods and his wife
says to him 'Joe, there's a leaky tap in the kitchen and the
toilet won't flush properly. Can you fix them?'

"'Hell no,' says Joe. 'Do I look like a plumber?'

"Next time Joe comes home, his wife says, 'There's a
short-circuit in the light switch in the living room. Fix it.'

"'No way,' says Joe. 'Do I look like an electrician?'

"Joe comes home again. The wife says, 'There's a squeaky
floorboard in the kitchen and a porch step is wonky. Will
you fix them?'

"'Are you kiddin' me?' says Joe. 'Do I look like a carpen-
ter?'

"Now, the fourth time the lumberjack comes home, he

looks around the house and everything's fixed. 'What happened?' he asks his wife.

"'Well,' she says, 'a handyman came around who said he could fix anything, and all he wanted as payment was some of my baking – a big cake – or some sex.'

"'What kind of cake did you bake him?' asked Joe.

"'Are you kidding?' says his wife. 'Do I look like Betty Crocker?'"

By that point, the gabfest was in gear, and all four men were giggling.

"I started my practice in a small town in Saskatchewan," said Doctor Dickout. "It's where I met my wife, Laura Short, actually. The local paper reported it as the Short-Dickout nuptials, but that's another story. This story's about gophers that were getting into the town churches. There were three denominations and the gophers were getting into them all and making one helluva mess. They put me in charge of a solution. So I went to talk to all three churches.

"The Catholic Church took the attitude that gophers were God's creatures, so just let them be. The Anglicans were for trapping the little beasties humanely, then taking them out into the country and releasing them. Of course, they wasted no time getting back into the church. The Baptist church had the best solution: baptize all the gophers, then they'll only come back to the church at Christmas and Easter."

"I haven't heard anything like that since Christ left Moose Jaw," said Phil. He was slumped against one wall of the beach house, his body languid, his mind bobbing on waves of contentment.

"If we're talking religion," said Neale, "would you rather be locked in a hotel room with a murderer or a Jehovah's Witness?"

"The murderer," answered Mike.

"Right," Neale congratulated him. "The murderer will only bother you once!"

"I've got one for you, based on the comedic rule of three," Phil put in. "What's the difference between a cactus, a carcass and a caucus?"

The others shook their heads.

"A cactus has a lot of pricks on the outside, a carcass is a dead body, and a caucus is a dead body with a lot of pricks."

Mike recovered from another giggle fit, then he said, "Last New Year's Eve I promised myself I'd do at least ten entirely useless and stupid things this year. Well, I voted once and I intend to vote again – that's two." He staggered to his feet and threw another stout log into the stove. "But right now I'm getting the munchies. I'll go up to the house and bring back some grub. You guys sit tight."

Dim Mak

Dim mak can have tragic consequences," the instructor said to the handful of students clustered around him. "So you have to be damn careful how and when you use it."

Gaston Ready and the others in the group had spent several years training at the Kung Fu Academy and were deemed ready to learn the death touch.

The ancient art of dim mak consisted of striking acupuncture points on the body to bring about illness, loss of consciousness or death. Depending on the strike and the force used, the victim's demise could be instantaneous or delayed. The early Chinese practitioners of dim mak manipulated the same vital points to revive their victims. Its origins shrouded in secrecy, dim mak gradually spread to other countries and influenced the development of karate and other martial arts in Okinawa, Korea and Japan. Inevitably, the techniques become popularized so that most of the modern martial arts systems included elements of dim mak.

Gaston's instructor had brought him into this group based on Gas's assertions that his motives for learning the death touch were benign.

"I doubt I'll ever have to use it," Gas said, "but these are dangerous times. I'm also thinking of going into security work. Never know when it might come in handy."

Following the stern caution to the group, the instructor used Gaston as his subject to demonstrate one dim mak strike. Immediately, Gaston felt his left arm go numb and effectively useless.

"The feeling should come back in a few minutes," his burly instructor assured him. "If I wanted to, I could've deadened that arm for days. Now, each of you is going to practise on me, and you're going to hold back. If I get hit too hard, you're out of the class. Understood?" He glared around the circle until he got a nod or a yes from each participant.

Gaston proved an able student and, buoyed by his success in this first taste of serious capability, he powered his way through the rest of the group class, with its emphasis on building strength and speed. The session ended with kicking and punching drills at ever-increasing speeds until the group collapsed, sweating and panting, onto the mats.

Showered and changed, Gaston headed up-Island on the Malahat Highway, through Duncan and up to Courtenay, where he booked in at the old Riverside Hotel.

The next day he caught the small ferry to Denman, then crossed that island to catch the next ferry to Hornby. Damn nice place, but hard to get to, he thought. *Warm climate, fertile soil, an excellent place to grow weed. But now I hear we've got problems.*

He met Neale Downe at his shack, which was tucked well back in the bush. "I got your message and would have answered by letter, only I didn't know how to spell bastard, you bastard."

Both men laughed. Gaston took a seat at the kitchen table while Neale cranked the tops off two cold beers.

"What in blue blazes happened to the crop?"

"Gone, kaput, fini," Neale replied, slamming his bottle down on the table. "Some sonofabitch tipped off the Mounties. Lucky I wasn't there when they swarmed the place."

"We've got contracts to fill and things could get nasty if we can't produce."

"We still have a bit of the finished product, but yeah, we need a lot more to hold up our end. I keep thinking that this rip-off would never have happened if I'd been content to stay on Texada Island. But no, I had to try to grow here. Would have worked fine, too, except for some busybody whistleblower who doesn't understand the first thing about pot. Likely believes all that horseshit about it being the violence-causing instrument of the devil, instead of a free-enterprise, high-profit business."

"So what are we gonna do now?" asked Gaston.

"Those goddamn cops owe me," said Neale. "So I was thinking, where can we get a ready-made supply?" Gaston just shook his head. "And the answer is – from the guys who from time to time have a lot of it."

"Who would that be?"

"The cops who stole it in the first place."

"The Moundies!"

"Who else?"

"You mean steal it back?"

"Yeah."

"Now there's something to think about." Gas's face clouded. "Hmm, I dunno."

"Look, I'm going to get some information from an inside source about when the Mounties are going to make a big seizure. Not just the plants, the processed pot. That's when we'll make our move."

"This source – "

"A guy I've known for a long time."

"Can you trust him?

"Yes, implicitly."

"This is the Horsemen we're talking about."

"No yeah-buts, we can pull it off if we plan it properly. How often do they get robbed? They won't be expecting it."

Neale handed a piece of paper to Gas. "This is the address of the incinerator they use to burn the product, as much of it as they don't use or sell themselves. Here's what I want you to do. Tail the cops from their Victoria headquarters to the incinerator. That'll give us a map of their route. Make some notes on places where we could hit the transport. Then check out the incinerator site. My information says it's run by the Capital Regional District, and it's the only place on the Island where they burn dangerous materials."

"All right, I'm in, but your plan better be good."

Finishing his beer, Neale said, "My guy's going to call next time they make a Mary Jane run. Then you can check out the route. Now, let's drive down to a great place I know, the Seabreeze, and have some supper."

"What's so great about it?" asked Gaston.

"The food, but mainly the management. A real character, name of Mike Fowler, is the innkeeper."

They entered the driveway to the Seabreeze Guest Farm and got out of the car. Several dogs came running to greet them. One of them, named Down Boy, tried to hump Gaston's leg.

"He really likes you," Neale laughed at the embarrassed Gaston. "Down Boy!"

"Damn strange-looking pack of dogs," said Gaston, pointing to one in particular.

"Mike tells me that one's a Mexican Careless. His father was a committee," Neale replied.

Mike hollered a greeting as they entered the dining room, where their host was playing the bass. "Have a seat, dinner's on in a few minutes."

Evelyn was on the piano and one guest was hooting on the trombone. Several others danced in the parlor. A goat walked in on its hind legs to join the party, then in came Down Boy, who edged over toward Gaston with a loving look in his eyes.

The music stopped and Neale introduced Gas to Mike.

"Does your dog do any tricks, other than try and screw the guests?" asked Gaston.

"You bet," said Mike. "Okay folks, your attention please. Dinner is about to be served and I'm going to ask Down Boy here not to sing God Save the Queen, along with the rest of us, before we say grace."

Down Boy obediently jumped up on the piano stool and faced the guests, who had taken their places at the big table. Mike plucked the opening bars on the bass as the guests began to sing. It took them a few beats to catch on.

"That's a smart dog," Gaston admitted to Neale. "And almost as horny as the goat."

After dinner, Mike sang one of his favourite oldies but goldies, You're Some Ugly Child:

You're some ugly,
You're some ugly,
You're some ugly child!
The clothes that you wear are not in style,
You look like an ape every time you smile,
Oh, how I hate you, you alligator bait, you,
You're the homeliest child I ever saw.
You're knock-kneed, pigeon-toed, and box-ankled too,
There's a curse on your family and it fell on you.
Your teeth are yellow, you got no fellow
You're an ugly child,
God, are you revolting,
You're some ugly child!

Down Boy tried to hump Gaston again and one of the female guests danced with the goat. For encores, Mike sang I Can't Get Over a Girl Like You, So Get Up and Answer the Phone Yourself.

When Gas got back from his trip, he told Ann to take a look in the vestibule. She saw a gift-wrapped package about a foot square and a few inches deep. Removing the fancy wrapping, topped with a bow no less, she saw it was a weigh scale, with an attached note: *This will take you from zero to 140 in less than 10 seconds. Love, Gas.*

Have You Seen Jesus?

After the crucifixion, Jesus might not have been able to walk on water because of the holes in his feet. Being a Canadian, Sal Vachon knew that Jesus *could* walk on water, but only in the wintertime.

One of the best Bible bangers in the business, Sal was popular among right-wing Jesus junkies, which was why he had been called out to a Kelowna parish on another temporary pinch-hitting job for the Seventh Day Absentist Church. Sal knew this was going to be a tough crowd for a stranger to preach to, but he believed the shortest distance between two people was laughter. He felt that by putting some fun into fundamentalism, he could jolt his listeners out of their complacency and into doing good. It was a dangerous gambit, to be sure.

Backed by a full gospel choir, Sal began his sermon, designed to put the odd back in God:

"Brethren, sistern and dearly beloved, at the last posting I had I was preaching a sermon, just like this morning, when the Devil came into the church in a burst of smoke and flame. He ran up and down the aisles and declared, 'Beelzebub's my name. I am the Devil incarnate and the ob-

ject of all your fears.' An old man stood up at the back of
that congregation and shouted, 'You don't scare me at all, I
been married to your sister for forty-eight years!'"

When the uncertain murmur had faded, Sal continued,
"So why did the Romans tear down the Coliseum? Because
the lions were eating up the Prophets! Now, as Christians,
we all think that the Ten Commandments should be more
widely disseminated throughout our society, in our homes,
our schools, in public places. But did you know that you
can't put up the Ten Commandments in a courthouse? You
cannot put up Thou shalt not lie, Thou shalt not steal or
Thou shalt not kill in a building full of lawyers and politicians. Why not, you may well ask. Because it creates a hostile work environment!

"Two farmers each claimed to own a certain cow. While
one pulled on its head and the other pulled on its tail, the
cow was milked by a lawyer.

"Which of us will get into Heaven? That is a question
that many of us ponder. When Einstein died and went to
the Pearly Gates, St. Peter said, 'Can you prove that you really are Einstein?' And Einstein wrote out a whole page of
his mathematical equations. St. Peter took a look and said,
'Okay, come on in.' Picasso died and went to the Gates and
St. Peter said, 'You look like Picasso, but how do I know
you really *are* Picasso?' And Picasso drew his masterpieces,
one after another, and St. Peter said, 'Well, all right, come
on in.'

"When Gerald Ford died and desired entry to Heaven,
St. Peter said, 'I'm sorry to have to ask you who you are.
Albert Einstein proved who he was and so did Picasso, and
so I have to ask you.'

"Ford took a step toward the saint and tripped over his
own feet.

"St. Peter smiled and said, 'Come on in, Gerald!'"

Not everyone in the congregation appreciated Sal's performance. Some sat in disbelief, others in disdain; but Sal
refused to be discouraged.

"These are the jokes, folks, and you *are* allowed to laugh in church. We were talking about the archangel St. Peter. I tend to think that at times he fulfills the role of a heavenly stand-up comedian, who would say to God, 'I know you're all-knowing, all-seeing and omnipotent, and yet for the knock-knock joke to work, God, you have to say "Who's there?"'

"Knock, Knock," Sal shouted, then waited, and finally a member of the congregation answered, "Who's there?"

"Owen."

"Owen who?" several people shouted.

"Owen the Saints Come Marching in!" said Sal. When others began to yell out other knock-knocks, Sal knew he had them.

"Knock, Knock," said someone.

"Who's there?" the congregation roared.

"Doris," Sal replied.

"Doris who?"

"Doris locked, that's why I'm knocking."

"Knock, Knock."

"Who's there?"

"Yah!"

"Yah who?" yelled the congregation.

"Ride 'em, cowboy!"

"A word to the women in the congregation," Sal chimed in. "What do you call a man who's lost ninety-five percent of his brains? A widower! If a man is speaking in the forest and there's no woman there to hear him, is he still wrong?" Several women shouted Amens.

"Now, I've married a few people I shouldn't have, but haven't we all? Marriage is based on the theory that when a man discovers a brand of beer exactly to his taste he should at once throw up his job and go to work in the brewery. But unless you can stand criticism, it's best to marry a virgin.

"When God created woman," Sal continued, "he gave her not two breasts, but three. The middle one was in the way, so God performed surgery. The woman stood in front of

God with the third breast in her hand. She said, 'What shall we do with this useless boob?' And God created man!"

The congregation really began to get into the action. One man came down the aisle with a joint in his hand and told Vachon, "It's not sinful to smoke pot, because the Bible says, Let there be grass!" Another handed him a hypodermic needle and a bag of white powder and told him that religion was the opiate of the masses.

Sal preached the lights out, and even tried out his healing powers by suddenly declaring with great religious fervour: "A hernia has been healed! If you're wearing a truss, take it off. It's GONE! I detect that several people are being cured of hemorrhoids as we speak.

"Remember, folks," said Sal, wrapping up, "there wouldn't be any atheists if there was no God. You can't take it with you, so if you put it in the collection plate, I'll see that it's sent on ahead."

Sal, gratified with the way the service had played out, eagerly acquiesced when the choirmaster asked to approach the pulpit for a private word. As Sal turned to face him, the choirmaster said, "Praise the Lord!" and let him have a meringue pie right in the face.

Sal wiped his face with his shirttail, licked his lips and said, "Good pie! May my tongue be equal to this task. The reason they say Lead us not into temptation is that it's so easy to find the way ourselves."

Turning to the main body of the church, he exclaimed, "Of all the wonderful congregations I've preached to, you are one of them. So, as Bugs Bunny used to say, That's all, folks. And thank you, Lord! Amen."

That afternoon came the de rigueur baptism of new converts by the usual method of immersion. Sal stood waist-deep in Lake Okanagan with his flock surrounding him, performing the rite in the name of the Lord. Sal grasped each new member by the head and waist and dunked him or her under water.

As the parishioner came up gasping, Sal would ask,

"Have you seen Jesus?" Invariably the convert would answer in the affirmative.

A drunk wandered out of the bushes beside the lake, stumbled into the water and came toward the assembled churchgoers.

Sal saw him coming and immediately thought, Now, here's a guy who really needs to be saved. He grabbed the drunk and shoved him under water, then brought him back up. "Have you seen Jesus?" he asked.

"No," spluttered the drunk.

Sal grabbed him again and this time he held him under for thirty seconds. "Have you seen Jesus yet?" he asked.

"No, not yet," the drunk replied.

Not willing to accept this answer, Sal grabbed the drunk again and this time held him under for well over a minute, until the crowd feared he might be dead. Sal brought the drunk back up and asked again, "Have you seen Jesus?"

The drunk, spluttering and spitting water, replied, "Are you sure this is the lake He drowned in?"

Nullis Nullitatum

A week's relaxation and recreation on Hornby had done wonders for Phil, who returned to Victoria with renewed vigor, albeit a few files behind in his caseload. He was happy to settle back into the routine of dealing with the slippery dictums of the law.

Its detractors referred to his field as the legal cheesecloth of abstract concepts, ambiguous words and ambidextrous principles. Phil agreed there was something in that premise, which was tantamount to, or approximated, the truth.

With faith in things nebulous, his clients were ever hopeful of a decision in their favour, whereas they were much more liable to get the thin end of nothing, sharpened to a point and then broken off. But when the chips were down and the last dog was being shot, Phil still wanted them to come out on top.

He plucked a file off the perilously tented stack on the side of his desk: an estate matter involving a trust to erect a monument to a testator's wife's first husband. The issue was whether the executor, her second husband, had to comply with the terms of the trust, as it seemed to him to be a waste of money.

Phil mulled this over as he perused the case law. His first thought was that marriage was like boxing, the preliminaries often more entertaining than the main event.

Then a second thought struck him – why not just advise the second husband that, instead of testing the issue in court, which would be expensive, he could simply erect a monument and have the inscription read, Oh, why did he have to die?

Phil's secretary, Wanda Fucah, buzzed him on the intercom to announce that a Ms. Thistle Fielgud was in the office and wanted to see him if he had the time. For Thistle, Phil always had time, because she certainly improved his mood.

She walked into Phil's office like a telephone operator – every line was busy. She plumped her pulchritude into the chair in front of Phil's desk.

"As I recall, you had the stiff in the hotel room."

"More than one, actually," said Thistle with a smirk.

"Did my advice work out for you? It was the best I could think of on short notice, considering the circumstances." In hindsight, Phil wasn't certain of the wisdom of his counsel.

"Not entirely, Mr. Figgwiggin," Thistle said. "I thought the police bought it for a while, but later they asked me to come down to the cop shop for further questioning. Then they said they could prove I was in the room when Luke died and that I'd better fess up to it."

"Did they indicate what kind of proof?" asked Phil.

"Well, I think it was about hair. A matron questioned me. She was really friendly and said she admired my hair. In the process, I think she got a strand or two.

"There could also have been some of my hair on the bed in Fitzhugh's room. I think they're comparing samples and are about to turn nasty and charge me with something."

"What are they going to charge you with?" Phil asked, spreading his hands. "And when it comes to the cops, frankly my dear, I don't give a damn." Phil grinned. He'd always wanted to use that line.

"Maybe murder!" said Thistle, turning pale as she spoke.

"Nonsense," Phil hastened to reassure her. "Where's the motive? There isn't one."

"Yes, but I had the opportunity, and I heard one cop say I screwed him to death."

Phil paused and looked at her. "You do have the capability, I'll agree, but why would you kill the proverbial golden goose? That argument would be *nullis nullitatum*."

Thistle squirmed in her chair. "What does that mean?"

"The epitome of all emptiness," Phil explained. "It would never fly in court, I'd see to that. They must have some ulterior motive to even suggest it."

"What are we going to do, Mr. Figgwiggin?"

"You and I will take the offensive, go down there together and find out just what they think they're doing and try to stop it."

"What about your fee?" asked Thistle. "I'm not exactly flush at the moment."

"Don't worry about it. I won't let you down. Let's just forget about money for now. But your concern about fees has triggered an old song in my mind. Want to hear it?"

"Sure, why not?" she said, wondering if her lawyer, who was past middle age after all, was losing his edge. Phil half sang, half recited the words:

Please don't burn our backhouse down
Mother says she will pay.
Brother's away on the ocean blue
And the cat's in the family way,
Father's gone and lost his job,
Things are pretty hard
So please don't burn our backhouse down
Or we'll all have to go in the yard.

Thistle laughed and felt herself relax. "You *are* taking my problem seriously, aren't you, Mr. Figgwiggin?"

"Of course, my dear, but that's not to say we shouldn't have a little fun along the way. We'll figure out how to get you out of this."

"Thank you," said Thistle. "I'm sure you know what you're doing. Someone told me you once debunked the law of gravity by proving Isaac Newton was never in an orchard."

"An exaggeration, Thistle. That's actually a quote attributed to George Bernard Shaw. At any rate, I appreciate your confidence and I'll set up an interview with – who did you say called you?"

"Detective Constable Colin Allkarz. Feels like he's creeping up on me, just like winter underwear."

"I'd better send someone to pick up that Fielgud dame," Allkarz to the desk sergeant. "Maybe I shouldn't have done it, but I gave her a chance early this morning to come in voluntarily."

"I just got a call from her lawyer. They'll be in to talk to you this afternoon. Figgwiggin said four o'clock."

"That's her lawyer?" asked Colin.

"Yeah."

"Okay, I'll tango with him, but I hear he'd give a dog's ass the heartburn."

Allkarz didn't share the opinion of some others on the force who persisted in pronouncing his name as Colon. However, he didn't see himself as an asshole. All he had done to earn the appellation was to fall asleep on the job. Not so bad in itself, as it could happen to anyone.

But in this instance, it had occurred when he was the only cop left on duty in lockup. All the others had been called out to halt a march on the legislature by homeless protestors. A prisoner's pals gained entrance to the cop shop and released all the prisoners. Worse still, they'd stolen all the toilet seats on the way out, leaving the police with nothing to go on.

As a result, Colin was desperate to obtain all the convictions he could in order to redeem his reputation.

"Just why do you want to talk to my client?" Phil asked when they were seated in Allkarz's office. "I thought you and I could simply discuss the circumstances of Luke Fitzhugh's death, which, of course, exonerate Miss Fielgud from any wrongdoing."

"She wasn't telling me the truth before, and we have evidence to that effect." Allkarz's shoulders were tight as he hunched over his desk in a combative pose.

"The truth is, why should she tell you the truth? Unless she was under oath, of course. She found herself in strange circumstances, but she did nothing wrong as a result."

"That's not what I think," countered Colin.

"You're trying to pin something on her that won't stick."

"She lied to me, which means she has something to hide."

"You should read H.L. Mencken on that subject, Detective. He said, 'It is hard to believe that a man is telling the truth when you know that you would lie if you were in his place.'"

"Let's cut to the chase, Counselor. Your client's guilty of something, and I'm going to make sure she's charged with whatever the Code will allow. For starters, we're charging her under Section 213, which bans communication between a known prostitute and clients in any public place."

"You're on a fishing expedition and no trout will be caught on that line of reasoning."

"Sez who?"

"Says me, and I hope you're listening."

Colin stared back coldly at Phil, then thrust a charge sheet across the desk. "There's also a charge of obstructing justice. She purposely interfered with and delayed our investigation of Fitzhugh's death. We're still considering second degree manslaughter. See how you like them apples."

Thistle's mouth felt like the bottom of a baby's pram – all piss and biscuits.

The Passing Parade

The distinctive strains of Glenn Miller's String of Pearls washed over Phil as he savoured a café au lait and pastry at Bogart's. The small downtown café's intimate atmosphere, filled with the usual business habitués, offered daily newspapers and yesteryear's swing tunes, along with lattes, mochas, cappuccinos and other ways to get a quick caffeine fix.

Tapping his fingers in time with the music, Phil figured if Miller were still alive, he would doubtless regret his 1934 composition Annie's Cousin Fanny, whose lyrics included the lines:

> You may know some girls called Annie,
> That are divine,
> But you never saw a Fanny,
> Half as pretty as mine.

Phil's grasshopper mind, killing time before heading to the law library at the courthouse, recalled a limerick:

> There was a cowboy named Tex

With very small organs of sex,
When accused of a rape
He was allowed to escape
Pleading *De minimus non curat lex.*

The Latin phrase meant the law takes no notice of trifles. Put another way, one need not use a steam hammer to crack a peanut.

Phil finished his java, stepped out onto Fort Street, then proceeded around the corner onto Blanshard, heading for the courthouse library. Who should he see coming toward him but an old reprobate client from times past, Myron Balloney, looking much the worse for wear. Some people thought Balloney was as shifty as a shithouse rat, the type of drunk who would split his thirst with you for half your beer; but the man had an undeniable charm.

"Haven't seen you for a coon's age," Myron exclaimed as he recognized Phil and shook his hand heartily. "Got time for a coffee?"

"Just had one, actually, Myron," Phil replied. "But I've got ten minutes, let's sit here and talk while you have one."

"Which I sure as hell need," said Myron as they sat down in the iron chairs outside another café. At Myron's request, the server brought him a cup of black coffee.

"Tell me what you've been up to," said Phil, knowing Myron was always up to something.

"Just came from police court," said Myron. "I told this young prosecutor I was feeling sick, and I sure was. I didn't feel like defending myself, so I called him over and said, 'Boy, I'd rather you withdrew this charge and save us all a lot of trouble, because there's no use going on with it.'"

"And he didn't buy that?"

"You can't expect things to be rosy in a courthouse, and this prosecutor says no, they would never allow that. So I'm in the docket and my case comes up. The charge is being intoxicated in a public place, and they figure they have me nailed to the cross. I only got out of the pokey last Saturday, and Tuesday I was drinking some beer and rye with a friend in a rooming house. I got drunk as a brewer's fart. Old Boozer, the warden at the jail, would really be proud of the one I tied on. I woke up in the hospital with a bandage on my brow.

"Then the cops show up and book me into the local constabulary on the aforementioned charge. And as I've said, I find myself up before the beak. You know, they should never let old jokers like that SOB on the bench. I wouldn't have minded his age and red-faced countenance if he only knew some law, and he doesn't. Say, Phil, what do you call a lawyer with an IQ of 75?"

"What?"

"Your Honour," said Myron with a laugh. "So I plead not guilty right off, naturally. Then the cop that picked me up reads in his evidence and says he found me in the can – bathroom, if you prefer – of this rooming house, lying on the floor where I'd fallen and bashed my head. That I was drunk I couldn't deny, but I stoutly maintained that this was no public place.

"The magistrate wouldn't buy that and had that convicting look about his demeanour when I told him, 'Okay, but I was the guest of Jim Conlay in that rooming house, and he is not provided with, for the goodly sum he pays for his lodgings, with a private can and bath. Therefore, he is forced by circumstances to use the can down the hall when nature calls – which he has a legal right to do, as the management provides that for the paying clientele.

"'Well,' I says, 'I was the guest of Jim Conlay and was using his can in his abode. Therefore, how can you rule that I was found drunk in a public place?'

"They adjourn court for a while and after they confer for about ten minutes, the magistrate resumes the bench. In the summing up, I'm holding staunchly to my case, and although at first he hems and haws, I told him, 'That's the law and, good bad or indifferent, by God, it's to be enforced,' I say, and in the end they withdraw the charge. I told that young prosecutor in the first place not to waste our time and that I really was feeling awful sick, but he wouldn't listen. I know you would have, Phil."

"A job well done, Myron, and I'm glad you no longer need my services. Gotta go. Nice seeing you again." Phil left him to finish his coffee.

Marcus Innes, the courthouse librarian, was an old school friend of Phil's. They went back a long way, and as part of their ritual, rehashed the time when they were fellow thespians in a Grade Four class play that would likely never be forgotten at their school. They'd each had a few lines to recite in that shades of Shakespeare effort.

Marcus was to say, "O fair maiden, I come to snatch a kiss and fill your soul with hope." Immediately following this, Phil was to say, "Hark! A pistol shot!"

The night of the play found the two boys very nervous, aware that their parents were in the first row. Finally it was time for Marcus to speak, and in his agitated state, he said, "O fair maiden, I have come to kiss your snatch and fill your hole with soap!"

Hearing this, Phil, even more upset, blurted, "Hark...a shitol pot! A postal shit! A cow shit – bullshit! I didn't want to be in this play in the first place!"

"What case brings you to the library today, Phil?" Marcus asked.

"My client, a pet shop owner, sold a lady a canary. Turned out it had a broken leg. Of course she complained, he failed to make amends and she's suing him."

"And you're defending? Seems cut and dried for the plaintiff."

"We're pleading that my client sold her a singer, not a dancer."

"Phil, you don't change," Marcus said, laughing. "Did you hear about the kidnappers who captured one hundred lawyers? They sent a note to the police saying, 'If our demands aren't met we'll release them one at a time.' Now get on with whatever you're doing and let me get back to work."

As Phil searched for the cases he wanted to cite in his defence of Thistle Fielgud, he thought about the strategy he planned to use. It was time to stop making hookers do business through car windows. Although it wasn't illegal to pay a person for sex in Canada, various sections of the Criminal Code were used by law enforcement to circumvent that fact. Phil believed that the country's sex professionals should have the freedom to conduct a legal business on private premises, to hire help and to advertise. Thistle's case could give him the opportunity to argue that proposition.

For instance, what was the intent behind the provision aimed at banning bawdy houses? It amounted to a situation in which prostitutes could not organize a brothel where they would be able to look out for one another and combine their resources to buy medical care, security or insurance. Phil felt his adrenaline surge at the inherent injustice and realized he was spoiling for a fight on the issue.

Go Figure the Odds

Neale Downe lived a bachelor's life in the boondocks of Hornby Island, a life that he didn't always find satisfactory. Men get horny – that's Victoria's Secret; men get lonely – that was Neale's problem, and accounted for two reasons why women bought giggle garters and romance refused to die.

Neale agreed with June Callwood, who had said, "Solitude is everyone's first friend, most pitiless foe, and best hope." Neale had certainly put his solitude to good use by making a good living growing pot, while disengaging his cognitive gears and allowing his imagination free play as he pondered the exigencies of life in the human zoo. As a result, he didn't have many friends.

Neale had grown up in a tough neighborhood, where one in four of his acquaintances was stupid, and another was boring. In his experience, the same ratio applied across the broad board of humanity. But he also realized that frequent intercourse with the wider world was vital if he wanted to keep his mind in health and vigour.

That's why he liked to visit Seabreeze, where occasionally he met some of the other two out of four people, who could comprehend satire, sarcasm or irony. Since Neale frequently indulged in all of these, he was often regarded as a cynic, a goofball or an aggravating wiseass who wasn't firing on all cylinders.

Right now, however, he definitely needed Gaston Ready, who had proven to be one tough cookie, though certainly no genius. Neale knew that IQ did not measure intelligence per se, but rather the capacity to process information, both verbal and nonverbal. Gaston could certainly do all of that and put it to good use, and for the purpose Neale had in mind, Gas possessed invaluable physical skills.

"Don't worry, Thistle, this fornicaboobery will pass," said Phil to his worried client as they sat once more in his office.

"What do they call them in Italy?" Thistle wondered aloud. "The paparazzi – I mean the reporters here in town. They pester me for interviews and the cops are likely watching me. I'm too high profile and the johns don't want to do business with me anymore."

Phil thought that over. "I've got just the spot for you. Go up to Hornby Island and check into the Seabreeze Guest Farm. I'll phone my new friend Mike Fowler who owns the resort and arrange everything. The place is scenic and quiet. You'll have a good time and also get some rest."

"You mean stay on my feet and off my back," Thistle said with a smile.

"Correct. You are out of the business until this case is resolved. At which time, I think you should use your brains rather than your beauty. You might even consider that good advice."

"I'll think about it. I've always figured it's better for a girl to have beauty rather than brains, because men see better than they think."

"Fowler wouldn't object if I told him who you were, but it wouldn't be fair to him if you don't act the goody two-shoes."

"They read the papers up there?"

"Maybe, eventually."

"So they could figure out it was me."

"Not if we changed your name."

"Good idea! Got any suggestions?"

Phil thought for a few moments. "How about Florence Ealing?"

"I like it. Okay, I've got my back to the wall, but I'm Florence Ealing until you get me off the hook."

When Colin Allkarz had first joined the Victoria police force, he had been unfortunate enough to be on duty at the main desk when Leo Tarde came into the cop shop to register a complaint. Colin was trying desperately to learn three things about being a cop: a bird in the hand will do you dirt; never deal with idiots, because you have to deal with them on their own level, and they're so good at it, they'll beat you every time; and if you don't expect people to be reasonable, you'll save a great many disappointments in life.

"What's the nature of your complaint?" asked Colin.

"Two weeks ago I was driving down Government Street," said Leo. "These two young girls flagged me down and asked for a ride home. Said they were broke and stuck downtown with no money. It was late at night and the bus service wasn't available. Being a trusting soul and a Good Samaritan, I complied.

"One of the girls got in the front seat and the other in the back, and we headed out toward Esquimalt. Pretty soon the girl in front started coming on to me. I couldn't drive properly with all that going on, so I pulled over into a side street. She took off her sweater and she wasn't wearing a brassiere. I admit I got a little excited and we began to wrestle around on the front seat."

"So what's to complain about?" asked Colin.

"The girl in the back seat picked my pocket while this was going on, and then they both jumped out and ran away, leaving me in the front seat with my pants down around my knees. When I checked my wallet, all my cash was gone. Cost me about two hundred and twenty-five bucks."

"That was two weeks ago. Why are you just reporting that this happened?"

"Because I wanted to catch them myself. So I went back down Government Street last week at about the same time of night. The girls were there again. This time I got their names."

"Which were?"

"Betts Zaroff and Annie Mahl."

"Don't tell me," said Colin. "You gave them another ride."

"Yeah, but this time I was smarter."

"How so?"

"I only had ten dollars in my wallet."

"So it's last week's theft you're reporting? Is that it? Why wait a week to come here?"

"Well, I went down there again last night and they wouldn't get in the car unless I carried more money."

From this encounter alone, Colin learned that some people are like slinkies. Not really good for anything, but they bring a smile to your face when pushed down the stairs.

At the Victoria headquarters of the RCMP, Sergeant Kenny Dewitt placed his meaty palms flat on his desk as he contemplated the constable standing stiffly before him. "But how well do you know this redneck source of yours? Can we trust him?"

"Well, Sergeant, as you know, I was undercover up in Port Hardy for quite a while. Too damn long, actually – and I've been meaning to talk to you about that.

"How well do I know the guy? He invited me over to his house for Thanksgiving dinner. He told his wife she'd ruined the meal because they ran out of ketchup. He wonders how service stations keep their restrooms so clean. He lost a tooth opening a beer bottle and he was fired from a construction company because of his appearance. He avoided arguments with his missus about lifting the toilet seat by using the sink."

"Okay, okay, sounds like you've gained his confidence."

"Just to be sure, I double-checked with another source. The pot's grown out in the Raging River and Three Lake Creek area and processed near Port McNeill. They're going to ship it down through the Inside Passage and the Strait of Georgia, passing through Trinconali Channel. If we use our boats out of Long Harbour on Saltspring, we could easily intercept them before they get to Prevost Island. We can track them by helicopter, too. I've taken a picture of the boat. It's a rental."

"Who owns it?"

"A guy in Winnipeg. Typical prairie boy, buys a boat out here, then gets tired of it. The marinas all over the Island are full of boats that are literally abandoned."

"Does the owner know what his boat's being used for?"

"Don't think so, no."

The sergeant rubbed his jaw as he thought. "There are places up-Island where we just can't detect the grow-ops. But this time we can put the boots to the cagey bastards, down here where we can get at them. Did you get an estimate of what the stuff was worth?"

"Yeah. They figure up to half a mil, a whole lot more on the street."

The Sergeant nodded, satisfied. "If we pull this off, there could be a promotion in it for you. I'm going to recommend you, in any case."

"Thanks, Sarge."

The Mounties continued to plan their operation to confiscate the huge shipment of BC Bud before it could get across the border into the Excited States, where the quality Canadian product was held in high esteem.

Callused Palms

Thistle Fielgud, in her new persona of Florence Ealing, arrived at Seabreeze on a Sunday evening. A man she presumed was the proprietor was marching around the front yard skirling on plastic bagpipes. His pants were rolled up and he'd fashioned a makeshift kilt from a plaid shirt wrapped around his waist.

Florence stepped out of her Volkswagen, recalling Figgwiggin's warning about islanders' eccentricities.

"Miss Ealing, I presume," Mike Fowler said, sketching a bow. "You're late. Do you have a note?"

"No. Nor do you, from what I've just heard."

"Touché. You and I are gonna get along, I can tell."

"Thanks for the musical welcome. That's a sad tune you were playing; maybe even pathetic. I haven't heard notes like that since my sister backed into a doorknob."

"Not my best instrument," Mike admitted. "Let's go into the house. My wife Evelyn will take you to your cabin. We'll bring your luggage around in a few minutes."

As they walked toward the building, Thistle took in the revamped farmhouse. An extension on one side proved to be a kitchen adjacent to a large dining room and parlour.

She was introduced to Evelyn and the two women headed back outside.

The sun was setting over Cape Lazo's sandstone cliffs, the lights of Comox airport glittering like rubies across the water. A cluster of lights illuminated Texada Island a few miles to the east and a wisp of smoke could be glimpsed near Powell River. Up and down the mainland shore, they saw the last lavender-pink glow of range upon range of snow-capped peaks.

"How did you come to get this place?" Florence asked.

"I was sick and tired of being a childless housewife in Burnaby," Evelyn replied. "I was determined to move. We spotted an ad in the paper for a guest farm called Seabreeze. Fifty-two seaside acres, a dining room, eight cabins, a boat, chickens and fifteen head of cattle. I said to Mike, 'Someday I'd like a place like this,' and he said, 'Why not now?'"

"Any regrets?"

"Not so far. My first choice would have been a teahouse in Stanley Park, but this turned out okay."

As Evelyn ushered Florence into a cheery but utilitarian cabin, Florence exclaimed, "It's spotless!"

"Thanks," Evelyn replied. "Usually, housework is something nobody notices unless you haven't done it. I love the place now, but it *is* one helluva lot of work. We've been slowly but steadily improving the property."

"What kinds of things have you had to do?"

"Well, when we first came here, the facilities were all of the outdoor variety – the pipes and plumbing fixtures that were supposed to replace the outhouses were lying around in heaps. The generator wasn't hooked up and there was no phone."

"I would have left the next day," Florence remarked.

"That's how we felt the first week, but we stuck it out."

"My law– ah, my friend Phil told me there was no ferry service when you guys bought the place."

"That's right," Evelyn said.

"So how on earth did you get here?"

Laughing at the memory, Evelyn said, "Mike got hold of a forty-foot war surplus boat and all our stuff got loaded in front. There was a noisy, and yes, stinky diesel engine under a deck canopy, something like *The African Queen*. We hadn't listened to any weather forecasts, and all we had to navigate by was a road map."

Florence shook her head in amazement.

Staring pensively out the window, Evelyn continued, "So we chugged under the Lion's Gate Bridge, rounded Point Atkinson and ran straight into a stiff nor'wester. Mike was incredible. He just set his compass to 250 degrees, then to 260 when we sighted the Ballenas Islands between Courtenay and Nanaimo. By then the wind and the sea were calm and the old boat took us right into the dock at Ford's Cove. The only trouble was, it was low tide. We were fifteen feet below the pier!"

"Did you have to wait for the tide to turn?"

"No, we got lucky – again. A car came down the hill and stopped on the dock. The driver was supposed to have a cherry picker for us, but he said he couldn't do it, I don't remember why not. So Mike cracked a beer and through the bottom of it, he spotted a fish packer with a crane on board. The skipper peered over the rail of his ship and said, 'You seem to be having a problem there.'

"Mike said, 'Yeah, I got this cargo down here and the wharf's up there.' Meanwhile, he's cracked open another beer. The skipper watched for a bit and said, 'I think I could get that cargo up there for a very low fee.'

"'What might that be?" Mike asked.

"'Well, maybe a case of beer.'

"Mike yelled back, "I'll throw in a bottle of rye!'"

"Great story," Florence said, laughing.

"Mmm. Then all the villagers came down with trailers and trucks and hauled us and our goods all the way here." Moving back toward the door, Evelyn said, "It's been a good life. We've kept our prices low, so we've had a steady flow of people all these years. We grow most of our own fruits and vegetables, and we've got animals for milk and eggs."

"Is there a lot to do here, other than sunbathing?" Florence wanted to know.

"Sure, you can take the rowboat out and go fishing, or hike. There are plenty of easy trails and it's a small enough island that you can't really get lost. Oh, and if you're a bird-watcher, there are cormorants, eagles, my favourite great blue herons, gulls of course, and pretty often you'll see sea otters or even a whale. Now then, Florence, supper will be ready within the hour. You'll hear the gong. Afterwards we'll have some homemade entertainment, some music and dancing. Don't be late, I've made a special dessert."

Florence was on time and pronounced the food exquisite. Evelyn had pulled out all the stops to create a gumbo from local seafood. The dessert was Moor in a Shirt, a concoction made from bread with the crust removed, whipping cream, butter and farm-fresh eggs, toasted and ground almonds, chocolate chips and a touch of almond extract. The ingredients were beaten with a fork, placed in a pudding mold, wrapped with buttered wax paper and heavy-duty foil, then immersed in a steamer for two hours.

"Ooh, this is yummy!" Florence said, helping herself to seconds.

Earlier, Mike had introduced the young man seated next to her as Neale Downe. At first he was rather tongue-tied and blushed when she spoke to him, but loosened up as the meal progressed. To make conversation, Florence inquired after his health, although he appeared in excellent shape.

"I've been clearing brush all day," Neale replied. "I feel stiff all over."

Like a trout rising for a worm, Thistle would have jumped on that line immediately, but as Florence, she couldn't touch it with the proverbial ten-foot pole. This dual personality bit's going to be tough, she thought.

"Any of these little rug rats belong to you?" Neale asked, glancing around the table and obviously hoping they didn't.

"No."

"Husband coming later?"

"Nope."

"How long you staying?"

"Two weeks, maybe."

"Hmm. The Seabreeze is more popular with families and couples. I show up about once a week for the food, but they don't get many pretty single women here. Nice change."

"Why thank you, kind sir," Florence replied. "And what else do you do when you aren't scarfing back this great food?"

"I'm what you might call a horticulturist. I live back in the bush and grow organic products."

"A farmer, no less."

"Yeah. How about you? What do you do?"

"I'm a diesel fitter in a pantyhose factory," Florence quipped.

Neale looked quizzical. "I don't...how does that work?"

"I hold up the pantyhose and say, diesel fitter."

Neale groaned. "Okay, you got me with that one."

After dinner, everyone gathered around the piano, with two guests sitting in on drums and sax. "I don't know if this band's gonna be fast, slow, or just half-fast, but this'll be a change from the big band 78 records," Mike said.

"The members of this little combo are all soloists in their own right," he continued. "If you don't believe me, just listen to us playing together. But right now I'd like to play and sing for you an old tune called Shanc." Mike grabbed his bass by the throat. "As in Bei Mir Bist Du, or as it's also called, The Bear Missed the Train:

The bear missed the train,
The bear missed the train,
The bear missed the train,
And now he's gone.
He got on at Penticton
Got off at Castlegar,

The train left the station
And now it's gone too far.
Oh, the bear missed the train . . .

"I could've been the world's greatest organist, if my
monkey hadn't died. My next number haunts me. I suppose
that's because I've murdered it so many times."

The two long dining tables were on rollers, and as the
band launched into a series of jazz standards, Evelyn and
Neale pushed the tables to the side of the room to provide
extra space for dancing. Not willing to miss the opportunity
to hold a beautiful redhead in his arms, Neale, with some
trepidation, asked Florence if she could put up with his in-
frequent attempts at tripping the light fantastic.

She looked him over as they danced. He did have a certain rural charm, and was not bad-looking to boot.

"I'm glad I have sore eyes," said Neale, "'Cause you certainly are a sight for them."

This guy is smitten, Thistle realized. After being a lady
of negotiable affection, she'd forgotten what it felt like to
be courted. Maybe she *should* rethink her career path. First
she'd have to turn down the role she'd been offered in that
porn flick, Not So Tiny Tim.

They danced out onto the wide veranda to the butch-
ered strains of I Had the Craziest Dream. The moonbeams
dancing on the waters of the bay seemed to match their
steps. Neale turned out to be a better dancer than Florence
had expected.

Morning broke with a singular beauty and Florence
watched the sun warm the sandstone cliffs. The sea was a
deep turquoise and the grass a bright green dotted with con-
tented cows. She breathed deeply, content with her memories of Neale gallantly walking her home after the dance.
She was having a truly wholesome good time. Still, she told
herself, I'm damned if I'm going to get bitten by any trouser
snakes on this island.

Two Little Flies

Tanya Hyde was a precocious pre-school kiddiwink who always seemed to be underfoot somewhere in the condo complex. Her parents were relieved when she went off to spent at least part of the day at school.

On this day she was wandering among the flowerbeds in the front gardens. Not only smart for her age, but also blessed with a prodigious memory, Tanya quickly picked up anything she heard from adults. She was singing a favourite ditty to herself as she played:

Two little flies they decided to roam
They packed their bags and they left their home
They flew away with a buzz and a hum
And they told their parents to kiss their bum.

Oh, one was black and the other was blue
One had a spot on his tra-la-loo
The other had a ring around his ring-a-rang-a-roo
Hi-ho the merrio!

They flew right over to the grocery store

And in through the transom right over the door
They oomped (Tanya blew a raspberry) on the bacon
and they oomped on the ham
And they didn't give a damn for the grocery man.

They flew right over to the burlesque show
And they took two seats in the very first row
And when the girlies came out to dance
The dirty little beggars they oomped on their pants.

Debating whether to walk or take the car, Phil stepped
into the elevator at the Whynan Beach Road complex. Already aboard was Isadore Shutt, a local would-be politician
with as little chance of being elected to Victoria's city council as the proverbial snowball in hell. Izzy suggested they
take the bus, because public transportation was a hot topic
in the city.

They found Tanya determinedly digging a hole in one of
the front flowerbeds with a garden trowel.

"How are your parents?" asked Isadore, privately wondering where they were.

"Mommy's coming soon, we're going shopping. Daddy's at work. I love my Daddy, he's such an asshole."

Must have heard that from the mother, or maybe her
grandma, thought Phil. "Are you going to plant some flowers here?" he asked.

"No," Tanya replied, still working the trowel.

"What, then?"

"I'm going to bury my goldfish," was the testy answer.

"Oh, too bad," Izzy commiserated. "Your goldfish
died."

"Yes," said Tanya.

"That's a pretty big hole you're digging for a little goldfish, isn't it?" Izzy commented.

"Not really," said Tanya. "My goldfish is inside your
goddamn cat."

Izzy, who hadn't seen his cat anywhere for the past two

days, looked concerned. To humour the child he said, "Well then, your goldfish will be up in Heaven with God."

"What would God do with a dead cat?" Tanya snapped, jabbing the trowel viciously into the ground.

At Phil's office, Wanda Fucah informed him that the crown prosecutor's office had served them with the charges against Thistle Fielgud in the Fitzhugh case.

Phil perused the multi-barreled document. Thistle was charged with manslaughter and obstruction of justice. The document also contained the much lesser charge of violating Section 213 of the Criminal Code, which banned communication between prostitutes and clients in any public place.

I'll kick their ass on 213, thought Phil. *And that manslaughter charge must be the idea of that crazy Colin Allkarz wannabe detective. If he'd studied law any harder he could have been a notary public.*

Phil was surprised the prosecutor's office had gone along with that bit of business, but he'd find out how serious they were before the preliminary. Allkarz likely figured the defence would agree to cop a plea on the 213 or the obstruction charge if the prosecution dropped the manslaughter business. Laying multiple charges was often the way the cops worked, even though it made for a lot of unnecessary work for the defence if they wouldn't play that game. Nil desperandum, thought Phil. *The game ain't over till it's over.*

Phil entered his inner sanctum and took the appropriate comprehensive copy of Halsbury off the shelf to refresh his memory on manslaughter. What about self-defence? Luke had been threatening Thistle with a blunt instrument with intent to cause bodily harm. However, he hadn't laid a finger on her, let alone anything else. The charge was a crock, only a happenstance and the Crown knew it.

The autopsy showed accidental death by heart attack. Was Thistle a *particeps criminis*, a party to a crime? No, fornication wasn't a crime. This wasn't even coitus interruptus. Any good judge would rule the episode to be a failure on the part of the deceased to consummate a fair fornication, and apply the 4 F's: Fitzhugh had only been interested in find 'em, fool 'em, frig 'em and forget 'em. The same description could just as easily apply to Thistle.

Thumbing through legal tomes searching for cases on point was not Phil's favourite pastime, particularly when one had to contend with passages such as: *The Supreme Court reversed a lower court ruling which had upheld an earlier decision by a circuit judge allowing an injunction which would restrain a Defendant from contesting an order to force him to show cause why he should not be enjoined from initiating a law suit.* No wonder laymen gave legal terminology a wide berth. Phil would happily put off his research until tomorrow if he hadn't already put it off until today.

While he was working his butt off with the law books, Phil figured he should also research the substance Fitzhugh had taken to enhance his sexual prowess. Phil discovered that the Spanish fly, found in the southern parts of Europe, was an emerald green beetle from the family *Moloidae*, about twenty millimetres long and seven wide. Up to five percent of its content was cantharidin, which irritated animal tissues. The crushed powder, a yellowish brown-olive with iridescent reflections, carried a disagreeable scent and bitter flavour. It caused inflammation in the genitals and subsequent priapism. The amount required was miniscule, and the difference between the effective dose and the harmful dose was quite narrow.

Ah, there's the hook on which I can hang the prosecution and that cop who's the main reason for all these charges. Can't trust him any farther than you can see up an alligator's ass in a dust storm at midnight.

The history of Spanish fly, a potent aphrodisiac, went back hundreds of years. Even Hippocrates had described its medical use. The Chinese used to mix it with human dung, arsenic and wolfsbane to make stinkbombs. In the 1670s, Spanish fly was combined with dried moles and bat's blood to make love charms. The Medicis had blended excessive doses of the substance with food to bring about painless death.

"The phone's ringing," Ann Kerzaway shouted to Gaston Ready.

"What'd you expect it to do, honk?" Gas shouted back. He was damned if he was going to get up from his easy chair.

"Wouldn't it be funny if the phone did honk?" Ann said from the comfort of her own recliner in the next room. "You'd end up with a horny phone."

"You'd like that, wouldn't you?" Gas said, finally getting up to answer the phone.

"Am I talking to Gaston Ready?" asked the voice on the other end.

"None other," Gas replied. "Who's this?"

"You were expecting a message, weren't you?"

"Yeah."

"There's a run leaving headquarters at three pm next Friday afternoon. Got that?"

"Yeah."

"Over and out." The caller hung up.

"What was that all about?" Ann, ever inquisitive, wanted to know.

"Gotta do some important business right away, is all. I'm setting the alarm for eight."

"You know, Gas, you're too damn secretive with all this phone business. Just don't get any ideas, like in this song I heard today."

"What song's that?"

Thanks for the memories,
The night that I came home
And you were not alone,
You said she was a nudist
Come in to use the phone,
Oh, thank you, so much.

Gas couldn't help chuckling. Ann never disappointed when he needed a laugh. He looked at her thoughtfully, then said, "I've gotta find a mission for you, Ann."

"Might be a good idea," she said, "because right now, we're looking at this ballgame through different knotholes. I have to do something. How about a version of Russian roulette?"

"How the hell do you play that?"

"You get six cobras in a room, you play the flute, but one of the cobras is deaf. Hey, what happened to my rim shot? That was a zinger!"

"How about a horselaugh?" Gas offered.

The Next Chapter

Each year when the Seabreeze milk cows calved, a number of the births took place out in the fields instead of in the barn. The Fowlers told their guests that whoever found a calf got to name it. No matter what the weather, every child and some of the adults would head out on a search that often lasted hours.

The calves were named after famous personalities, like Princess Margaret and Pierre Elliott Trudeau. Two or three years later, they'd be served up as dinner. The guests would be startled to hear that they were eating Astrobert or Anthony Armstrong Jones.

That year, the menagerie included a stray calf that two teenagers had found and dubbed Madonna. Mike fed her from a pail with a nipple attached.

Madonna adopted Mike as her surrogate parent, following him everywhere, often accompanied by the goat, the dog and the cat. One day Mike took out the trombone and blasted away as he led this animal parade to the general store to pick up the mail. They were a huge hit, and the pied piper bit became a ritual.

Mike was on his way to the barn to feed the animals,

singing a song inspired by his hard-won experience in tending cattle:

> Oh, give me a home, where the buffalo roam,
> And the cowboys all work till they drop.
> Where all of the cows lie flat on their backs,
> And that brings the cream to the top!

Mike had noticed that Neale Downe was showing his
face at the Seabreeze much more frequently than in the past,
no doubt due to the presence of Florence Ealing. On this
sunny late afternoon, he observed the two of them playing
gin rummy on the shady porch. They waved at him and he
waved back.

Everything's great when you're young and healthy, he
thought. *You'll even get a bang out of a screen door.*

Mike continued around the house and stepped in
through the back door just as the phone rang.

"Is that you, Mike?"

"Yeah. How're ya doin', Phil? Still feelin' fine?"

"I never cease to be amazed at the strength of my weak-
nesses. And you?"

"Don't sweat it. Health nuts are going to feel stupid
someday, lying in hospitals dying of nothing."

"So how's that special guest of yours?" Phil asked.

"I figured that's why you were calling," Mike said with
a chuckle. "Well, she's a looker, Phil, and you and I know
that sometimes means trouble. But she's turned out to be
a class act. The other guests think she's a peach, and she
and Ev are like sisters already. She's been helping with the
chores, and Ev's trying to convince her to stay longer. Don't
worry, nobody here's gonna guess how she earns her keep
in the big city."

"Sounds good," Phil said, sighing audibly. "Just let her
know I called, will you? No news on her case, but I'll be in
touch when the hearing date is set."

"Roger that."

As Florence shuffled the cards, she asked, "Exactly where on the island is your place?"

"It's kinda deep in the woods," Neale replied. "Hard to get to. You go about a mile past the Co-op Store junction; there's a bad dead-end road to the left. I leave my truck at the end of that and walk through the woods to my cabin."

"How big is the, whatever you call it?"

"It's a large backwoods farm," he replied. By calling his shack a cabin and the adjacent marijuana grow-op territory, which he didn't own, a farm, Neale knew he was stretching this depiction like a flea's ass over a bathtub. But what the hey, he now had plans that would put him in the money and allow him to become a respectable businessman.

"I'd like to see your farm sometime," said Florence.

"No you wouldn't," Neale replied hastily. "It's a dump. Just deal the cards, and try to give me a good hand for a change. I don't want to get skunked."

"I may have been born and bred in the city," said Florence, realizing she could have worded that remark a bit differently. "But you must have some farm animals to feed, like Mike Fowler here, right? Any pigs?"

"No pigs," Neale answered.

"Why not?" asked Florence.

Neale thought that over for a moment, then said,

Mary had a little pig,
She kept it fat and plastered,
And when the price of pork went up,
She shot the little bastard!

Florence laughed, but pressed her point. "How about other animals? Sheep, lambs?"

Neil picked up his cards and recited:

Mary had a little lamb,
Her father shot it dead,
Now it goes to school with her,

Between two loaves of bread!

Neale finally had a good hand. He kept a six, two sevens and an eight and threw a ten and five in his crib. Now if he could get a good cut, he might even win the game.

"Well, how about pets? Dogs, cats?"

"Large cats can be dangerous," said Neale.

"Maybe, but a little pussy never hurt anyone," Florence replied, just to test Neale's reaction. She paused, then said, "Perhaps I should rephrase that."

Neale blushed but said nothing.

"So, can I come and visit this dump of yours?" asked Florence, as Neale cut the cards to reveal a nine.

"No. There's really nothing to see, honestly. I may be selling it soon, anyway. I'm planning on moving up in the world."

"Sex is non-existent on Hornby," Denton McCarr, a guest at the Seabreeze, complained to Mike.

"Why do you say that?" his host asked.

"No privacy in the cabins, if you've got your kids with you."

"I can fix that," Mike offered. "Boys like to sleep in the hay in the barn. I'll lay that on for tomorrow night and announce it at breakfast."

McCarr clapped his host on the shoulder. "Thanks, Mike."

Things were all set to go in the McCarr cabin the next night, but his wife couldn't stop fretting about her child and sent Denton to check on him. Denton, in the grip of grab-ass fever, rushed into the barn and quickly made sure the boys were all right. In his subsequent hot-to-trot haste to get back to the cabin, he kicked over a container of oil used to fuel the stove that kept the calves warm. Denton spent the rest of the evening cursing his luck and mopping up oil.

Florence decided to explore the island by car. She came to

a place that fit the description of the road leading to Neale's place, and decided to pay him a visit whether he liked it or not. Sure enough, there was his truck parked in a rudimentary roundabout at the end of the short, rough road.

She got out of her car and walked down a narrow path through the woods. The scene reminded her of the old fairy tale of Snow White and the Seven Dwarfs. She said aloud, "It's a little-known fact that Snow White had twins. And the reason for that is that only one of the dwarfs was Dopey!" She looked around her. She was no expert on rural life, but this looked like no farm she'd ever seen.

The path ended in a small clearing, where a small, nondescript shack hugged the forest edge. She knocked.

Neale wasn't accustomed to visitors and he opened the door cautiously. She sensed his disapproval of her visit, as he didn't immediately smile.

"I thought we agreed you wouldn't come here," said Neale.

"Curiosity," Florence said breezily. "Your description seemed odd, and now I can see why. I don't see any cultivated land."

"Okay, so I'm just a recluse."

"What crops are you growing here? As if I couldn't make an educated guess."

Bowing to the inevitable, Neale swung the door wide open and ushered her in. "Come on in to my humble abode and we'll discuss it. I can even offer you a drink. Beer is proof that God loves us and wants us to be happy. That's all I've got, unless you'd rather have coffee."

The place was clean, though sparsley appointed. "Judging by the outside," said Florence, "I thought maybe the place had gone to pot. If you weren't going to tell me anything, what wouldn't it be?"

Neale cranked the tops off two Molson's, placed them on the table and grabbed two glasses from the cupboard. "Would I be right in assuming you wouldn't say anything about something, even if you did know something?'

"Could be."

"Okay, I admit it. The place *has* gone to pot. But I don't grow it near here. I'd like to ask you one question, though, Florence."

"Which is?"

"How disappointed are you to find out I'm in the marijuana business?"

"I've had my share of tokes, and I think the marijuana laws are stupid. Besides, if you can hide some income from the feds, more power to you. I'm certainly not about to criticize grow-operators. So it'll be like I was never here."

Florence accepted the beer Neale had poured for her. She took a welcome sip, then continued, "But I'll bet it's a tough job, and risky to boot."

At Neale's nod, she added, "Oh well, I figure Easy Street's a blind alley. And if life were easy, we'd be bored to death."

They chatted a while longer, but Florence could tell Neale was still uncomfortable. She took her leave, saying she had to get back in time for the weekly hayride.

As Florence disappeared down the trail, Neale thought, Of all the crappy shacks in the world, she walks into mine.

The Chapter after That

So many potentially peaceful evenings were spoiled by newspaper stories like the one Phil was reading – a reprint from the *South China Daily Express*. Phil, a news junkie, was convinced that in-depth stories and unflinching examinations of US foreign policy were more likely to be found in the British, European or Asian press. The *Express* item, picking up on a story first broken by a Lebanese magazine, carried details of a complex arms-for-hostages scheme hatched by US government officials.

Michael Ledeen, a part-time National Security Council employee, had first proposed selling arms to Iran, then at war with Iraq, in the summer of 1985. President Reagan had approved the sale that July. In return, Iran was expected to put pressure on Hezbollah terrorists in Lebanon to release the thirty hostages they had been holding in that country since 1983. The plan failed, as only three of the hostages were freed.

The proceeds from the arms sales were deposited in a Credit Suisse bank account controlled by Lt. Col. Oliver North, also on the NSC staff. They were later funnelled to right-wing Contra insurgents in Nicaragua, who were hell-bent on destabilizing that country's democratically elected Sandinista government.

Phil could feel his blood pressure rise as he read of the CIA's involvement in the affair.

On fifteen flights early last year, the Southern Air Transport Co.'s big-bellied aircraft took 406 tons of cargo into El Salvador's Ilopango military airport, the principal trans-shipment point for Nicaraguan insurgents. Southern Air, based in Miami, is a wholly owned CIA subsidiary using the cover of a civilian airline.

The CIA's role in supplying the Nicaraguan Contras might have remained a secret but for an occupational hazard: on Oct 5 last year a transport traced to Southern Air was shot down over Nicaragua. The sole survivor, Eugene Hasenfus, quickly told interrogators that he thought his mission was backed by the Central Intelligence Agency.

Phil thought the CIA should run a TV game show called Spot the Liars. *These are the clowns that run covert American foreign policy and various false-flag operations. Undercover companies do the CIA's dirty work, the CIA does America's dirty work and Americans don't much care about anything, unless you forget to salute the Stars and Stripes.*

Snatching up another paper, Phil's attention was drawn to the headline: *The CIA is seriously ill.* The article stated that the Agency's director, William J. Casey, had resigned following surgery for a malignant brain tumor. His replacement, Robert M. Gates, had served as Casey's deputy since the previous April. Gates was first informed of the possible diversion of funds to the Contras that fall, but was more concerned about the risk of the Iran-Contra operation's discovery than about the scheme's illegality.

On the comments page of the same newspaper was an opinion piece predicting that, barring a miracle, George H.W. Bush, a former head of the CIA, would be America Inc.'s "suit" after Ronald Reagan left the White House.

Bush will pour out unaltered from the Oval Office almost anything that's poured into him, just like James Baker and the rest tell him to do.

George Bush was a man ill at ease with words, the writer maintained, as if aware they might contain meaning and thus arouse expectations.

As he read, Phil nodded in agreement. Politicians are like diapers, he thought. They needed to be changed often – and for the same reason. His long-standing fear was that incompetent and dangerous "suits" like Bush would try to establish a corporate police state in the US, and that whatever happened there would slop over into Canada.

Phil threw down the newspaper in frustration. On his way to the kitchen to refresh his coffee, he got detoured to the front door to answer a knock. There was Doggerel Don again, sheaf of paper in hand and asking him to read and comment on another verse. Sighing inwardly, Phil invited Don in, settled him in the wing chair opposite his own, then sat down to read Don's latest opus.

A civil engineer one day as we shall now relate
Met with a fatal accident and thus did terminate
And found himself to his surprise before the pearly gate
Conferring with St. Peter as to what would be his fate.
St. Peter checked his record and spoke awhile with God,
Then told our engineer he wasn't destined for this sod
That he would have to go below and on hot cinders trod
He wasn't deemed as worthy, which seems a little odd.
The engineer soon found that Hell was not a bowl of ice cream
And he promptly showed the Devil that with the proper team
They could use the extra heat and turn it into steam
That would run the mighty turbines that would make the place a dream
And with all that thermal power, air conditioning was a snap

And with robot fire tenders it quickly closed the gap
Between Heaven above and Hell below. Hell was now a
tourist trap
And soon became the favoured spot on everybody's
map.
When God called down to check how the engineer was
doing
And the Devil showed to God the great things then ensuing
God said, "Since these are good things, his passport
we're renewing
And do not try to stop us or you'll find that we'll be suing."

Now this was something novel that must surely give us
pause
That God would seek the law courts to settle His own
cause
Would a lawsuit really make the Devil pay out through
the schnozz?
Or was the case transparent as a piece of flimsy gauze?

And then the Devil looked at God and gave a great big
smile
"I really do not think you'll sue; for one, it's not your
style
And secondly, you passed him by; you couldn't win a
trial
And where in Heaven are the lawyers that would help
you file?"

Phil commented, "It covers two important subjects,
Don, the law and religion. The major premise is that all lawyers are scurrilous, greedy crooks. You know the type of
joke – what's black and white and looks good on pinstripes?
A pit bull on a lawyer! Or, how many lawyers does it take to
change a light bulb? How many can you afford?

"That's how most people see lawyers, and we've been the butt of thousands of jokes. But what few people get is that lawyers stand between them and a fascist government. Every person is innocent until proven guilty by a preponderance of evidence against him or her. The burden of proof is on the prosecution. They have to prove guilt, and the accused is entitled to the benefit of reasonable doubt. The underlying concept is that it's better that ten guilty men go free than one innocent man hang. The rule of law, habeas corpus, that kind of thing.

"There may be some bad apples in the legal barrel, but we don't advise our clients to lie, and if a lawyer himself lies to the court, he's subject to disbarment."

"So we're going to have a serious discussion for a change," Don said.

"Can't hurt occasionally."

"You think we should be worrying about the government and the police more than the state of the legal profession? But don't the police and government stand for law and order?"

"Supposedly, but they're far more interested in order than in the law. It only takes ten steps for a country to turn into a police state."

"Care to enumerate them?" asked Don.

Phil, still steamed over the articles he'd read earlier, was happy to vent. "First comes the invocation of a terrifying enemy, either within or outside the country, to justify increasing restrictions on basic freedoms. The general public is easily led into this trap, by the way. Second, you create a gulag."

"A what?"

"A secret prison system outside the rule of law, where torture is routinely used to extract 'confessions.' In the beginning, they'll only jail those scary people of a different race or colour. Then they'll start hounding the dissenters, the protesters, anyone they regard as a shit-disturber. To carry out these activities, they develop a thug caste."

"Say again?"

"A bunch of scary young men who are immune from prosecution. You dress them up in identical uniforms, like the brown or black shirts they had in Europe in the Thirties, then set them loose to terrorize the citizenry in the name of restoring public order. Next you set up an internal surveillance system, where the secret police spy on ordinary people and encourage neighbors to spy on each other.

"Then follows arbitrary detention, then you target key individuals in your opposition, like Mussolini or Goebbels did."

"What else?"

"You control the press. Create a steady stream of lies to pollute the news. Muddy the waters till citizens can't tell the real news from the fake, and thus they gradually give up their demands for accountability. Any dissent is called treason; any attempt to get at the truth is espionage, for which you can be executed. There goes free speech."

"That must be ten reasons," Don said, by this point regretting his visit. Phil had the bit in his teeth and there'd be no stopping him now until he ran out of wind.

"The final step is the suspension of the rule of law. It could all happen by a process of erosion. So to come full conversational circle, Don, that's what lawyers are trained to try to prevent."

"That's a great theory, Phil –"

"No, these aren't theories, they are the proven facts of history."

"There's also the religious aspect to the poem," Don said in an effort to haul back on Phil's reins.

"Pure unadulterated bullshit, of course, shoved down our throats from early childhood onward. What kids really need is the truth. What they get instead is a baloney sandwich."

"Yeah, the belief in a God. That there's this good guy up in the sky somewhere that watches over us, and this bad guy down below that lashes out with punishment if we commit a sin."

Phil nodded. "Once they've drummed those cockama-mie ideas into you when you're young and impressionable, you'll believe anything they tell you. You're told your dead parents are up in heaven, where they watch over you and ask God for favours to help you here on Earth.

"Picture this scene," Phil said, a glint of amusement in his eye. As quickly as his ire had erupted, his quirky sense of humour now reasserted itself. "A deceased parent says to God, 'My kid plays for the Alberta Bullshippers and he'd re-ally like to win Saturday's game against the Southern Ontario Cornholers.' God says to him, 'I just had some people in here asking for Ontario to win. What am I supposed to do? Tell your kid, the team that raises the most money for the church will win the game. It would also help if your kid broke the leg of that ace Ontario fullback in the first quarter.'"

Don laughed. "That's the kind of thing we get from that itinerant preacher, Sal Vachon, up in the penthouse. He's depriving a village somewhere of an idiot."

"Well, now, think about it, Don. Sal's not as dumb as the congregations he preaches to. Some of them have hit the rock bottom of stupidity and are starting to dig. They don't question anything. Our experiment in democracy could be destroyed by erosion. These people just accept the status quo, especially the utterances of anyone in authority, with-out thinking critically for themselves."

As he got up to leave, Don said thoughtfully, "I was reading recently about A. A. Milne. You know, the writer who created Winnie the Pooh and Christopher Robin. His father used to tell him that the third-rate brain thought with the majority, the second-rate brain thought with the mino-rity and the first-rate brain thought for itself.

"There were facts he could teach his son, like how to solve a quadratic equation, but where there was uncertain-ty, where opinions differed, he'd have to think and decide for himself. He also said the largest, most fundamental and most vital area of uncertainty lay in what one believed about God."

"I haven't heard it put better than that," Phil admitted as he escorted his guest to the door and said good-bye.

Don means well, Phil said to himself. *But as someone once said, "Show me a poet and I'll show you a shit."* Phil believed that the writing of more than seventy-five poems in any fiscal year should make the author the central figure in an ass-kicking contest and be punishable by a fine of five hundred dollars.

Rampant Technicolour Horsefeathers

Neale Downe stared out the grimy window of his hermit's lair, the cadence of his thoughts echoing the drumming of the rain on the giant cedars beside the shack.

In Neale's mind, there was no contest between alcohol and marijuana. If you just wanted to get stupid or blotto, lose control and risk committing rude shenanigans, felonies or violent crimes, then booze was the answer. But if you yearned for a quiet, unassuming high that allowed you to be thoughtful and relaxed, then the substance of choice was cannabis.

Man made hard drugs and alcohol, Mother Nature made marijuana, so which was best? Pot didn't cause moral decay or make you want to fuck strangers.

Sure, Neale had thought about getting it on with Florence Ealing, but marijuana had nothing to do with that. It didn't make you mean, give you a hangover, make you punch out your mate or abuse your children. And it was a big help if you were terminally ill.

"So what the hell's the big deal?" he said aloud to no one in particular, because he was alone in his shack.

Neale walked out to his truck and drove in to the Co-op Store Junction to use the pay phone.

"I'll meet you in the beer parlour of the Riverside Hotel in Courtenay," he said to Gaston Ready in Victoria. "Save you a couple of ferry trips."

"Fine by me. See you there around two. I've got the information you wanted," Gaston replied.

The Riverside operated as a meeting place for Hornby Islanders waiting for the next ferry. As they sipped their first beer, Neale, in no hurry to get down to business, told Gaston stories about Seabreeze, including Mike Fowler's trials in trying to supply the guest farm.

If Mike needed something in a hurry, he only had to call the Riverside's beer parlour to say he needed someone to bring back ten pounds of round steak. It always arrived. He could get anything he wanted that way, except beer.

"They always promise to bring the beer back," Neale explained to Gas. "But then they take the booze cruise from Denman Island, and by the time they get to Mike, there's no beer left. He says, 'If this was the army, these couriers could be charged with insubastabordination!'"

"So how's he get around the problem?" Gas asked.

"Some of the islanders make their own beer, so he gets some from them, or makes his own. They even make potato champagne, if you can believe it.

"They're a different breed over there, let me tell you. One guy had to go to Courtenay for a medical check-up, and he knew he'd have to give a urine sample. He stopped in here and got drunk before heading off to Courtenay. He had the presence of mind to fill the mickey bottle with urine in advance, but he was drunk enough that he chugged the contents of the mickey, too."

Gaston's nose wrinkled and he put his beer glass back on the table. "Okay, so I got the message from your informant. I tailed the van carrying the pot from Moundie headquarters up-Island over the Malahat toward Duncan. Just this side of Duncan, they turned left onto Allenby Road. Then left again onto Koksilah Road, then onto a no-exit lane, a really crappy road that swings north. The incinerator's only a few miles up that road, three or four minutes max."

"Did you find a good spot for the hit?" asked Neale.

"Yeah. There's a small stream about a mile in. There's lots of brush where it intersects the road, so it's a good place to hide. There's also a little place for cars to pull off."

"Good. So what's the escort like for these shipments?"

"There were two young cops, and they didn't look to be on the ball. They've probably done this run so many times they've gotten sloppy. I doubt they'd ever expect their load to be hit."

"Fine. Now, how do we stop the van without tipping them off, and get them out of it?"

"I waited till after they'd burned the stuff. It was near quitting time and they went back into Duncan, started dunkin' doughnuts and trying to get friendly with the waitresses."

"Horny young guys, eh?"

"You got it."

"We can make use of that," said Neale, stroking his chin as he envisioned the scene. "How about we get some female help?"

"I'm getting your drift," Gaston replied, "and I have a coupla gals in mind."

Phil Figgwiggin, just back from his morning constitutional walk, opened his mailbox on the way through the vestibule and extracted several letters. Looking them over as he ascended in the elevator, he spotted one with a Hornby Island return address. Inside his condo, Phil poured himself a glass of orange juice and sat down to read Mike Fowler's letter.

Dear Phil:

We've finally decided to sell the Seabreeze operation. We're still only charging sixty dollars for a double occupancy cabin, while our competitors get well over a hundred. If we raise our rates, we might attract a new crowd, but they'd probably want better amenities. So after thirty years, I've had it. Why? Because I've literally been dipped in dingleberries and I'm getting out of here. We have an offer to buy at a very good price and I want you to handle the legalities of the sale. It's time for the eagle to shit so we can retire to Victoria.

What was the final straw that brought on the decision? I'd been partying during the evening and I'll admit I'd had one over the eight and was considerably inebriated. Something in the lane stirred. Was it a bird stirred? I thought, and I stumbled out to investigate. Out by the barn there's a pit where I dump all the manure. I got disoriented and fell in. Up to my waist, in fact. I was stuck, couldn't get out, and I quickly found out that urine ain't the opposite of you're out.

I yelled, "Fire! Fire!" People came running, pulled me out and cleaned me off. Then they asked me why I'd yelled fire. I said, "Would you have come if I'd screamed, 'Shit!?'"

This isn't a crock of shit, Phil, and if you think it is, then go shit in your hat and pull it down over your ears. If you think I don't know shit from Shinola, you're mistaken. The word shit comes from an Olde Englishe word, scitan, and its use has multiplied excrementally. Now it's one of the most-used words in the language, and that's no ape, pig, buzzard, owl, whale, dog, chicken, turtle, rat, cat or bat shit, let alone the ever-popular bullshit!

I'll phone you to let you know when I'm coming down and we can set up a time to meet. In the meantime, I've been trying to improve my literary education by reading some of the classics, like Mammaries of Things Past and From Here to Maternity.

By the way, Neale Downe's been asking me about Florence Ealing, that gal you stashed here for a few weeks. She took off and I don't have her forwarding address. Downe's in love, the poor bastard, plus I detect he has other problems on his mind.

That's all for now.

Your friend,

Mike Fowler

Not Their Ducky Lay

Obadiah Hawke, an indefatigable optimist, was a native of the Nootka Nation, whose people had long navigated the Inside Passage. He knew it well, especially its upper reaches, and could handle any type of boat. His buddies called him Tommy, or Tom.

His mate of longest standing was a Métis named Pierre "Spokey" Wheeler, inevitably dubbed Spoke because of a nervous speech problem. He tended to anticipate and switch sounds within a word or among words, especially when under stress. Tom could always understand him, though.

"That's the second time in the last hew towers that helifuckingcopter has pissed overhide. Don't you find that a little strange?" Spoke remarked as their boat chugged along.

"We're gettin' down inta civilization," Tommy replied. "There's a lot more air and sea traffic in these waters, including all the BC Ferries runs."

"Just the same, if that chopper shows up again," said Spoke, "we should think about taking some evasive action. We're damn near there, and it'd be too bad if we got caught now. A turd in the hand is worth boo in the bush. I mean a herd in the band is worth two in the bush."

"Come again?"

"I said, a hand in the bush is worth two on the bird."

"I know you said something," said Tommy, smiling to himself. "I thought you said a push in the bush is worth two in the hand."

"You've got a dirty mind, Tommy."

"And you worry too much, Spokey," Tom replied. "By tomorrow night we'll have finished the trip and be down in Seattle with our three favorite things."

"Remind me what those are."

"Lobster tail and beer."

"Good. But right now, I've got some stomach trouble. I gotta make a run for the soil it teat and shake an enormous tit."

When the copter passed overhead again, Tommy took Spoke's advice. The morning fog lying off Prevost Island had still not dissipated, and he headed the craft into it, figuring to stay out of sight for as long as possible.

"It's as thick as sea poop," said Spoke. "Let's leave no stern untoned to get this job done."

"There's a little creek runs into a bay right along here. I'll take a look at the map. We'll run in there and hole up for a while before we make the final run through Swanson Channel. When we see Stuart Island, we're practically in Yankee waters."

"Then to the drop-off near Rock Harbor, and it's our ducky lay!" Spoke added.

They ran in the fog for a short time, but it soon began to lift as the sun rose higher in the sky.

"Do you hear that?" asked Spoke.

"What?"

"There's a boat headed this way."

"Yeah, I do now, and at speed, too," said Tom. "Let's get into that bay." He turned the boat hard to port and opened up the throttle.

Too late. The Mountie speedboat out of Long Harbor in Ganges, Salt Spring Island, was on the job as planned, and their backup was a Coast Guard gunboat. The vessels came out of the thinning fog with lights flashing and sirens wailing. Someone aboard the RCMP boat fired a rifle at the fleeing smugglers.

"I thought I heard a thostle pit," yelled Spoke, over the roar of the boats. "I mean a thistle pot. Damn it! Can we outrun them?"

"No way."

"Well, can we beat them to the shoreline?"

"Yeah, we can do that much."

"Then give 'er snoose. What did one shepherd say to the other shepherd, Tommy?"

"What?"

"Just what I'm saying to you now: Let's get the flock out of here!"

As the boat came alongside the bank of the creek, Tommy slowed, reversed and cut the motor. There were 440 ten-pound bags of pot on board, and they each grabbed one as they leaped ashore and made a run for it, reluctantly leaving a small fortune on the boat going to pot and the Mounties. Tom and Spokey figured that by taking a bag each, they could salvage something from this fustercluck.

"The best planned lays of mess and mime oft go astray," yelled Spoke, as he and Tommy thundered through the bush. "But now our whacks are to the balls."

"You can say that again," said Tom. "I wonder who tipped them off? I don't like to swear, but I'm really p.o.'ed at the g.d. SOB who did it."

"I thought we were pretty fart smellers," said Spoke, "and that by this time we would've been in some pub raising a tankard of ale in a toast to the Deck and Doochess of Kunt and our dear old Queen, Rictoria Vagina."

"And we still might do just that if we can find a way off this island. Not to worry, Spokey," said Tom. "I know one of the few guys who live here."

In every military outfit, quasi- or otherwise, the dogsbodies all have to take their turn in the barrel, as it were. The cult of the Royal Canadian Mounted Police was no exception.

At the end of January that year, a Vancouver man charged with possession of drugs for the purpose of trafficking had appeared in court in Victoria, seeking to be released on bail. He was alleged to have swallowed several condoms full of hashish oil, and the authorities naturally didn't want him to get away until they'd had a chance to recover the evidence.

The prosecutor and the defense lawyer agreed that the accused should be released on bail, but not until he'd had three bona fide bowel movements. The court ruled that each of these momentous events was to be closely monitored. All movements were to be deposited in a chamber pot under the scrutiny of a member of the RCMP, so that the content of the excrement could be examined.

The judge asked the accused whether he would consent to the procedure, and defence counsel replied in the affirmative. Then the judge asked the defence lawyer, "Do you realize what this will do to the poor Mountie that has to do the monitoring?"

"What do you mean, Your Honour?" counsel inquired.

"You're going to turn him into a stool pigeon," replied the judge.

Chief Detective "Rocky" Glen Acorn decided this important bit of investigative police work should fall to someone who aspired to the detective squad, in keeping with the idea that such aspirants should start at the bottom. The lucky candidate was Constable John Potts, who was instructed to check each movement minutely and tabulate the relevant evidence.

"But sir," John expostulated, "why me? Couldn't we bring in a medic–"

"Now Potts, don't be a shit-disturber!" Acorn ordered. "Your surname made you the only logical choice. Just regard this as potty training."

His fellow constables were unanimous in their support.

They gathered around him and encouraged him with a
rousing fight song:

> Alakazoo, alakazam,
> Son of a bitch, goddamn
> Highty, tighty, Christ almighty,
> Rah, rah, shit!

John didn't really want to plunge into action, but he had
no choice. The condoms were recovered and at trial, the
accused was convicted. Potts won kudos from his superiors and months of ribbing from his peers: "John thinks his
shit doesn't stink." "He doesn't know whether to shit or go
blind." "Hey John, wipe that shit-eating grin off your face."

Then they regaled him with the story of the frog and the
eagle. A frog laments aloud that nature has not granted him
the ability to soar in the sky like a bird. An eagle, overhear-
ing the amphibian's complaint, swoops down and offers the
frog a ride in the sky. "Just crawl up into my asshole and I'll
take you for a spin," promises the eagle.

The frog gladly complies, and the eagle flies up and up,
eventually reaching an altitude of ten thousand feet. At this
point, the frog pokes his head out of the eagle's anal passage,
looks at the ground far below, and gulps, "You wouldn't
shit me now, would you?"

The Musical Riders made sure their seizure of 438 ten-
pound bags of high-quality processed grass, worth approxi-
mately half a million on the market, was widely publicized.
They needed all the positive media attention they could get.
The weed was delivered into safe custody at Victoria HQ
and placed under lock and key, together with more minor
drug seizures. The quantity in storage was now huge, re-
quiring destruction by the usual method of incineration.

Monday morning's posted assignment roster tasked
John Potts and his buddy Joe Kerr with loading and deliver-
ing the grass to the Duncan incinerator site.

Another Mountie constable, a recent arrival in Victoria from the BC Interior, made a note of the assignment and called Gaston Ready.

Getting the Hang of It

Thistle Fielgud sought out her lawyer two days after her return from Hornby Island. She complained to Phil that she hadn't even unpacked her bags when she got a call from Allkarz, who was putting pressure on her again.

Phil urged his client to sit, then asked Wanda to bring in some coffee. As they waited, Phil tried to put Thistle at ease by asking about her holiday.

Not willing to be deflected, Thistle replied, "It was a nice break, Mr. Figgwiggin, but here I am back in the soup again. What're we going to do?"

"It's my fault, unfortunately," Phil answered. "Because of the advice I gave you when I was heading off on holiday, the prosecution can prove you were in Fitzhugh's room. But in your statement to the cops, you said you hadn't been inside the room at all."

"It seemed like a damn good idea at the time," said Thistle emphatically, "so don't blame yourself."

"I was in a hurry when you called," said Phil. "I didn't foresee the possible consequences of my advice, or that the cops, in the person of that dingaling dorkbrain Colin

Allkarz, could be so determined as to try to pin a murder on you."

"So will I have to go to trial?"

"That depends on how strong the prosecution's case is. We'll find that out at the preliminary hearing. That's where they have to lay out the evidence to support their case. Then the judge decides whether there's enough evidence to warrant a trial. I'll try to get the charges thrown out at that point."

"Fine, but what if we end up having to go to trial? Will I have to testify?"

"The basic strategy is that if you're guilty, you take a jury, if innocent, then you take a judge. You're innocent, Thistle, so we'll choose trial by judge alone. Also, you look like a sweet young thing, and you are innocent, so it would likely help to put you on the stand in your own defence. But we'll make that decision later."

"But won't the court hold my profession against me? I could be tried and found wanton."

"Not likely. Let's just put it this way – you could be good for nothing, but never bad for nothing."

"So I'm to play the demure hooker with the heart of gold who's been led astray by evil companions, is that it?"

"You got it, my dear. Let's just say a call girl catering to men of wealth or high social standing."

"That does sound a little better."

"We'll deal with that when we get to it. For now and just for the hell of it – because we've had a hard day – let's have some good clean dirty fun." Phil got up and stepped over to the window. "I'll ask you some questions," he said, "and you give me some answers, just to see how young and naïve you can be."

"Okay, shoot."

"Where are you from?"

"Eyebrow, Saskatchewan."

"That's a pretty small place, isn't it? Was there any prostitution there?"

"It was so small, the only prostitute there was a virgin – me!"

"And I suppose Come Again was written on the back of the Welcome sign. So why did you come to Victoria?"

"I wanted to be a city girl."

"Why was that?"

"Because farm hands were too rough."

"How is a virgin like a balloon?"

"One prick and it's all over," Thistle quickly replied.

"What do they call the useless piece of skin attached to a penis?"

"A man."

"How is sex like a bank?"

"You've got me there," Thistle replied.

"Maturity yields increased interest, and there are substantial penalties for early withdrawal." Thistle hooted.

"What makes a cannon roar?"

"You'd roar, too if you had your balls shot off," Thistle replied, still giggling.

"What's the cause of the population explosion?"

"Too many fucking people!"

"How many Calgarians does it take to screw in a lightbulb?"

"Calgarians don't screw in lightbulbs. They screw in hot tubs."

"What do you call an Eskimo who's a Peeping Tom?"

"An optical Aleutian."

"Okay, one last question. Why is a high-priced call girl like a defence contractor?"

"That's easy. They both charge $1,000 for a screw."

"Very good, Thistle, but you do understand we don't want you to be so flippant in court."

"Certainly not, Mr. Figgwiggin, but that was fun."

"By the way, I just had a letter from Mike Fowler, the guy who runs the Seabreeze."

"He's quite the character. I had a really good time there."

"But you left early, didn't you? Do you mind telling me why?"

"I'd rather not talk about it."

"Would it have anything to do with a person named Neale Downe?"

Thistle moved uneasily in her chair, a surprised look on her face. "Why do you ask that?"

"Because Mike said Downe was asking where you'd gone and how he could contact you, er, Florence. Mike even said the guy might be in love with you."

Phil detected sadness in her eyes as she answered, "I liked him, but that was a situation that was going nowhere. He doesn't know what I do for a living, or that the cops are accusing me of fucking a guy to death. He doesn't even know my real name. And I want to leave it at that, if you don't mind."

"Of course. I can see how your situation might present problems for any relationship with this fellow."

In condo 206 of the Whynan Beach Road complex, Gaston and Ann had been having it on in spades. She had offered her honour and he had honoured her offer, and all night long it was honour and offer.

In the morning, as Gaston gazed at her voluptuous figure, he said, "You know how we've argued about you feeling left out of my business and not having anything to do?" At her nod, Gas went on, "Well, I've got a job of work for you."

"Glad to hear it. What do I have to do?"

"I was just thinking that with your looks, you could stop a truck."

"Thank you. Figuratively speaking, I hope."

"No, literally. That's the job – to stop a truck."

Ann sat up in bed. "What are you talking about?"

"Next Friday we're going to heist a truckload of marijuana on a back road up near Duncan. It's going to be driven by two young and horny Mounties. You and another gal are going to be on that road in a supposedly broken-down van, and you're going to ask the cops for help. Think you can pull that off?"

"Sounds easy enough," Ann replied, not even questioning the legalities. She'd known for some time that Gas wasn't doing charity work when he was away from her. Once she'd figured it out, she'd been surprised to find herself quite happy to live off the avails of whatever schemes he was running. "Who's the other woman?" She asked, smiling at how the question sounded.

"Name's Helen Hunt."

Ann considered this for a moment, wondering if she should ask how Gas knew Hunt. "Okay, so we're going to hijack a Mountie truck full of pot?"

"Right. And it's a really big load, a lot of it ready to smoke. You're always saying we need more dough."

"Yeah, it costs more to be poor nowadays than it used to. Who else is involved?"

"Just me and a guy whose name you don't need to know, but he has access to inside information and he's worked out the whole job."

"You're on then, Gas. I'll do it. Thanks, honey," she added, caressing his face. "I was really getting bored. At least I certainly was last night – if you get my drift," she said with a smile.

The Law is an Ass

Neale Downe's mouth stayed shut, but inside his head he kept talking to himself. He was aware that thinking could start innocently enough, but when the process got too heavy, it could ruin a person's life. *Maybe I should become a recovering thinker, join Thinkers Anonymous and try to avoid thinking at all.*

Once again on his favourite topic of marijuana, Neale groused internally about the court-ordered penalties for various pot-related offences. He knew the laws pertaining to drugs, and proudly scoffed at the ones he didn't like. Whereas he might agree with those concerning the hard drugs governed by the Food and Drugs Act and the Narcotic Control Act, he disagreed violently when bureaucratic dunderheads included marijuana in the list of prohibited psychoactive substances.

Possession of a narcotic, if a summary offence, carried a penalty of up to a thousand dollars and/or six months in jail. In the case of indictable possession, the maximum sentence was seven years.

First offenders were usually tried summarily, rather than by indictment, at the discretion of the Crown, which really meant whether the cops liked you or not, so the only crime was in getting caught.

Trafficking in a narcotic, or possession for the purpose of trafficking, and this included marijuana, was technically punishable by life imprisonment. If you imported or exported a narcotic, the minimum penalty for a first offence was a seven-year jail term, and the sentence could not be suspended. The maximum penalty was life.

In certain circumstances, the court might suspend the sentence for possession of a narcotic or drug, depending on the character of the accused, his background and the amount of the substance involved. Those were the laws, even though they were seldom fully applied, because even the courts knew the law concerning marijuana was an ass.

In Neale's opinion, the police and the politicians hadn't learned a thing from Prohibition. How could you explain to young people why nations that spent billions on war materiel and nuclear weapons were still trying to outlaw marijuana? And because it was illegal, a great many people were making a living from it, himself included.

Do-gooder types would say a citizen's obligation was to obey the law and work to change it; but Neale's attitude remained that he was not committing a crime, just being civilly disobedient.

So why not make one big score and then no more?

In any event, Neale was beginning to long for a less risky lifestyle, with maybe a wife, kids and all that jazz thrown in. And not just any wife. He couldn't stop thinking about Florence, remembering how pleasant her vivacious company had been and imagining how nice it would be to hold her in his arms and stroke her beautiful red hair.

Doggerel Don McGraw was chuffed. For years he had toiled in the footsteps of his hero, Robert Service, the man who had documented the fatal shootout in the Malamute Saloon between Dangerous Dan McGrew and the Stranger from the Creeks. Now Don had received an invitation to lecture at the University of Victoria where, as the saying went, the freshmen bring a little knowledge in and the seniors take none away, and knowledge therefore accumulates.

His seminar, aimed at aspiring creative writers with a prurient bent, was to be on the history of dirty verse, at which he was apparently considered an expert.

Don's plan was to begin with modern verse and work his way back to Chaucer and the ancients. He planned to include works by Shakespeare, Jonathan Swift and Alexander Pope. *Perhaps I could start with Sprightly Suzanne.* Rhyme and metre played an important role in ribald humour, and this was a prime, relatively recent example:

Suzanne was a girl
With plenty of class
Who knocked 'em all dead
When she wiggled her

Eyes at the boys
As girls sometimes do,
To make it quite plain
That she wanted to

Take in a movie
Or go for a sail
Or hurry on home
For a nice piece of

Cake, with some ice cream,
Or a slice of roast duck,
For after each meal
She was ready to

Go for a ride
Or a stroll with some hick
Or with any young man
With a sizeable

Roll of big bills
And a pretty good front.
And if he talked right,
She would show him her

Little pet dog,
Who was subject to fits,
And maybe she'd let him
Take hold of her

Little white hand
Or hug her real quick,
And with a sly smile
She would tickle his

Chin while she showed him
A trick learned in France
And would ask the young fellow
To take off his

Coat, while she sang
Of the sweet Swanee shore,
For, whatever she was,
Suzanne was no bore!

The Lord will provide, thought Sal Vachon. *But at the moment, he's behind in his payments. I've got to hit the Bible trail and make a few bucks.* So thinking, Sal set to work on the draft of a new sermon. He riffled aloud through a series of gospel themes.

"Dearly Beloved, what is it that I've come to say? Here are my thoughts. Let them folks who don't want none, have memories of not getting any. O joy to the world – and let that not be their punishment, but their reward. Don't be sitting there at eighty-five in your rocking chair saying, 'Well, I could've. . .' If you're ever going to amount to something, now's the time to do it.

"I'll tell you one thing, friends: anything you're doing now that's not leading you toward your desired goal in life – what are you doing it for? You all come up with these excuses, like 'One of these days . . .' Forget it! I believe that if everybody excelled to the height of what they enjoyed doing the most, then some of you would all be doing the same thing. I'll not pursue that thought, it's not on a proper plane. O joy to the world! There are many ways to experience life. Yes, yes, experience it to the fullest. Life is like a tin of sardines – we're all of us looking for the key.

"When I was a young man – just about as young as some of you here tonight – I used to love celestial, happy sounds and good things. But if you're always hung up on good things, how are you going to recognize something bad? Good and bad are relative concepts, you know. Dualities. What's a duality, you say? A duality is like good and bad, Heaven and Hell, love and hate.

"Population control is a big issue all over the world now. People are screaming about it, hollering about it. Some people are for it, some are against it. Actually, I'm for it and against it. Now here is a soul-searching thought – I wonder how many of us are mistakes? I know I was. Population control is a good thing to talk about, but I thank God my parents were ignorant of it.

"On the other hand, if we take population control too far, one day there won't be any people around, and then the folks who haven't made friends with animals are going to be awfully lonesome. That's one to think about, because some of you like to hunt. I'm not putting you down for it, even though I've always said it isn't right to render the animating force out of an animal with some kind of a weapon, such as a gun, unless the deer is trying to attack you. There's no sport in shootin' a deer. They look at you with those big eyes.

"Another thing is trees. Trees are just trees to us. But to birds, trees might be considered home. Doesn't that just grab you? Little old birds flying away up there, nesting in their homes. The bird says, 'Home, home!' He or she doesn't know how to say 'Timber!'

"Everybody's got a place somewhere, except folks who don't have a place, and they just seem to wander around on other folks' places . . . The mind is beautiful and we can think about a whole lot more than we can get. This is an untold joy. What is an untold joy? Well, that is a joy untold.

"Now, I don't believe there is such a thing as a mistake, and I don't go along with accidents. I think they're just premeditated carelessness. There now, tell that to somebody that don't care.

"And now for a few more random thoughts. You can't hurt a drunk, which is why some people think it's godly to drink. I think Goliath could have taken David if he hadn't been stoned. Finally, gratitude is riches and the worst I ever had was wonderful. God bless you all. Amen!"

A Trap of Boobies

On Friday afternoon, the two ossifers of the Canadian Moundies, John Potts and Joe Kerr, were approaching the Malahat, the only highway out of Victoria going up over the hump to the northern part of Vancouver Island. John was driving. Joe, the taller and older of the two, was ostensibly in charge, in that he did less work than John – a usual sign of authority. It was a warm day and the air conditioner in the van was blasting cold air.

"There's one helluva draught in here," said John, unaware he had forgotten to do up his fly. The radio played a country tune, mostly whining and complaining.

I was drunk the day my mum got out of prison,
I went to pick her up in the rain,
Before I could get to the station in my pickup truck,
She got runned over by a damned ol' train.

"I bet when he went to get his pickup truck, the battery was dead," John commented.

"Hope they play something more cheerful soon," said Joe, staring out the window.

The radio broadcaster was not about to oblige, playing some achy-breaky numbers instead: You're the Reason Our Kids Are Ugly; If the Phone Don't Ring, You'll Know It Was Me; and I Don't Mind Goin' Under, if It'll Get Me Over You.

"Turn it off," Joe ordered.

"Okay. Say, how are you getting along with the new female recruits, Iona Bond and Rhoda Dendron?"

Joe snorted. "The Dickless Tracys? Not so hot. No sense in trying to date them. But here's something positive. I got permission from the chief nut, Acorn, to park the truck at Duncan division and bring it back Monday."

John brightened considerably at the news. "Good on you, Joe. Means we can spend the weekend up here in new territory."

"Exactly."

"I hear there's a couple of good night spots and a big dance on Saturday night. Maybe we'll get lucky and pick up a couple of hot chicks."

"Potts, I bet you don't know the difference between a slut and a bitch. You don't, do you?"

"Okay, what *is* the difference?"

"A slut sleeps with everyone. A bitch sleeps with everyone but you."

"You know I can't remember jokes too well, but there were a series of those, right?"

"Yeah, like what's the difference between a magician and a line of chorus girls?" Smirking, Joe supplied the answer. "The magician has a cunning array of stunts. Another one was, what's the difference between parsley and pussy? Nobody eats parsley."

"So how about we pick up some pussy the first chance we get?"

"And it wouldn't hurt our chances if we were to borrow a bag of the cargo, would it?" Joe could usually get his brother officer to follow his lead. "Before it gets consigned to the incinerator. Pity to burn it all."

"Now, hold on a second," John protested. "A whole bag would be too dangerous. Where would we keep it? And if we got caught, we'd be goners from the Force or working someplace where it's colder than the hairs on a polar bear's bum."

"You've got a point. But maybe one of the bags gets torn and we take only enough for the weekend."

"Yeah, that could happen, all right."

At one time, the town of Duncan had been even smaller, and before that, there had been no Duncan at all. Those days were gone and now there was a plentiful supply of Duncan.

Gaston Ready turned the stolen vehicle off the Allenby Road onto Koksilah and then up the dead-end lane that led to the incinerator. The remote location ensured the local dopers couldn't get a noseful of the funky smell that continually emanated from the place. With Gaston were Neale Downe, Ann Kerzaway and Gas's other recruit, Helen Hunt.

The women had dressed to bring a smile to any man's face and a tilt to his kilt. They knew that the pursuit of women is the engine that drives the train of civilization. Birds and whales had it easy because they got hot and bothered only once a year. Human males however, seemed to be horny 24/7.

The heist crew was counting on the young Mounties to like their women big: big hair and big breasts, a jiggling assortment of C and D cups tethered beneath tight-fitting cotton tops. In case the cops turned out to be ass men, the women had also donned hip-hugger shorts and a mini-skirt respectively, with thong underwear.

The main expense for the job had been the rental of good wigs. Ann became a redhead and Helen stayed a blonde, but with longer hair. Ann's shorts were so tight she looked like she had been poured into them and forgot to say 'When.' You could read the embroidery on Helen's panties: *Help! I need resuscitation.* High heels and lots of leg were de rigueur, together with an attitude big and brassy enough to stop a truck.

A short way up the lane, near the stream, they parked the van so that it blocked the right side of the road, and Ann stood at the front of the vehicle, which had its hood up. She was ready to jump into the left lane so the approaching driver would have no choice but to stop.

Neale took a position in the bushes by the side of the road and pulled a balaclava over his face. Gaston went back up the lane a few hundred yards and did the same. He was to come up behind the vehicle when it stopped.

They didn't have to wait long for their quarry.

"You were so ugly when you were a baby, they had to hang a pork chop around your neck to get the dog to play with you," said Joe Kerr, by way of general conversation as they swung onto the Koksilah Road.

"Oh yeah?" John shot back. "If you look up ugly in the dictionary, you'll find your picture in the margin."

They continued to insult each other to pass the time as they turned into the lane leading to the incinerator.

"Lord love a duck, John, do you see that!?" Joe suddenly exclaimed.

A stalled van blocked one lane, while a gorgeous red-head stood beside it, frantically waving them down.

"We're not supposed to stop," John said, but he applied the brakes nonetheless and rolled to a stop some twenty yards short of the sexpot occupying the center of the road.

"Looks like her van broke down," said Joe. "I'll go check it out."

As he approached the woman, Joe was aware of nothing but tits and teeth, as she welcomed him with a big smile. "Officer, am I glad to see you! I hope you're mechanically minded. Maybe you can tell me what's wrong with this stupid old van."

Joe feasted his eyes on the lovely crumpet and remembered what he and John had been planning for the weekend. "I guess it can't hurt to have a quick look."

As he walked forward, another gorgeous girl stepped

out of the van. "I'm Charlotte," said Ann, "and this is my girlfriend Harriet. What's your name, officer?"

"Uh, well, it's Joe. Glad to meet you, girls. I'd better take a look at the motor." Joe proceeded to do just that.

John watched from the driver's seat of the truck.

Helen waved and sashayed a few steps toward the truck, beckoning John to come out. He hesitated, but couldn't refuse the offer. He opened the door and stepped down.

Gaston came out of the bushes and quietly ran up behind John, grabbed him by the shoulders, spun him halfway around and delivered a dim mak strike to the cop's throat. Potts dropped to the ground like a felled ox.

Helen ducked into the van and grabbed a pad of chloroform from the back seat.

Ann bent closely toward Joe, her boobs in his face as he searched the engine for loose wires or whatever might be wrong with the vehicle. Her nearness wasn't helping his concentration.

Neale emerged from the bushes and ran toward Joe. Kerr caught a glimpse of a hooded figure, rudely brushed Ann aside and went for his gun. Unfortunately, he wasn't an old Western gunslinger, not even a Gene Autry. It generally took a Mountie several seconds to get his sidearm out of his holster. Before Kerr could draw, Neale was on him like ugly on a gorilla, and they got locked in a ding-dong dust-up. Ann plunged into the fray and tried to kick Joe in the gonads as he spun to the ground. She missed but caught him in the arse with the pointed toe of her shoe.

Joe was hurtin' for certain, and violent language and angry shouts ripped and reverberated through the bucolic air. "Help! Mayday!" Joe yelped, then changed his mind and shouted, "John! John, it's a trap. Drive outa here. Get the hell out with the truck." But John was hors de combat in la-la land.

"Freeze," screamed Joe, trying to apply his police training. "You whoreson bastards are all under arrest!" But no one obeyed and only the birds heard the cacophony.

Gas joined in, and they overpowered the deputy-do-right, but not before Joe had torn off Neale's balaclava. At exactly that point, Helen slammed the pad of chloroform over Joe's face as the two men held him down.

When Joe had stopped kicking, the little gang dragged him back to the police vehicle, removed the keys from John's closed fist and unlocked the rear compartment of the truck. Gaston climbed behind the wheel, coasted to the side of the road behind the van and told the girls to start transferring the processed bags of pot into the truck.

Gas checked to make sure John was still breathing. He was happy to have learned to pull his dim mak blows enough to cause only unconsciousness. He had no desire to become a cop killer. Neale and Gas administered chloroform to John Potts, then wrestled both limp bodies into the front seat of the police truck. They cuffed the officers with their own handcuffs and left them there.

When the van was fully loaded with the loot, Gaston pulled a U-turn and hightailed it from the scene of the crime. Their mission accomplished, the robbers' joy was unrefined, and they headed for the hills like big-assed birds.

There was a short pause, then a longer one. The two merged together so you couldn't tell the difference. Ann spoke up, "Where to now?"

"We get back down over the Malahat before someone finds those jokers and brings them around," said Gaston, checking the speedometer to see that he was traveling at the speed limit but no faster.

"Then what?" asked Ann.

"Its best you girls know as little as possible about that," said Neale. "You go home, lie doggo and act normal until we finish this deal. We have to sell the stuff and stash the money. It'll take a little time, because I'm waiting to get some information before we make the sale. Once it's all over, we'll pay you two off. Don't worry, it'll all work out."

"It better," said Helen, who wasn't as trusting as the other three.

Ann removed her make-up and wig, then put on a pair of horn-rimmed glasses. Helen discarded her own wig and pulled on a pair of slacks. Soon they bore little resemblance to the highway sirens Charlotte the Harlot and Harriet the Chariot.

Boundless Faith

Doggerel Don scratched at the seat of his Donald Duck pajama bottoms as he shuffled into the bathroom for his evening ablutions. The jammies were a recent gift from his doddering mother who, being well into her second childhood, seemed determined to make Don revisit his. But even in this, Mother knew best, and Don had been wearing the garment for several nights.

On this particular Monday, as he flushed the toilet, his mind was full of ribald limericks he might use in his university seminar later that week. One he particularly liked was:

There was a young lass from Madras
Who had a magnificent ass
Not rounded and pink,
As you probably think;
It was grey, had long ears, and ate grass.

Don was crestfallen when he dropped his toothpaste on the bathroom floor. "Oops," he said as he bent to pick it up. But that's when the idea for a new poem came to him. He rushed into the den to put pencil to paper:

Now Joseph was a pious man, his faith in God sublime
And so it was no wonder that he sought Him all the time.
And every night upon his knee to Heaven he raised his arms
And cried to God, "Oh help me, I'll never do what harms
For all I ask is, think of me when the lottery wheel is spun
And let me win the jackpot so that I may have some fun."

This was his daily practice and it mattered not a jot
That the Lord had failed to answer him by giving him the pot.
So every night he gave his plea, his faith was strong and bright
But from the Lord no answer, until one fateful night,
The thunder roared, the lightning flashed, then came a Sepulchral Voice:

"You are a faithful servant but you don't leave me much choice.
"You have to give me lots more help, there are things that you must do,
"I know that I'm all-powerful and all those things are true,
"Like that I can part the waters or bring a locust swarm
Or create a second Ice Age or keep the waters warm
But I don't see how I'm to help to seek your name and pick it
"You've got to meet me halfway, Joe, and buy yourself a ticket!"

Doggerel Don had won second prize in the previous year's National Dirty Poetry Contest. This had depressed him no end, as he felt his filthy, foul, rotten and raunchy poem was the indisputable winner. He phoned one of the judges, who agreed that Don's poem was totally devoid of any redeeming social value. Still, at the last minute the judges had received an entry that made Don's look like a nursery rhyme, which was why that other poet had secured first prize.

"I'd like to learn from that poem," said Don, "please read it to me."

"No way, Jose!" said the judge. "The RCMP tap my phone. They'd record it and I'd be charged with inciting pornography and put in jail for a long term."

"Then send the poem to me," Don entreated.

"What?" screamed the judge. "They often open our mail – some court order or something, obtained by the League of Decency or maybe the IODE – I might get a life sentence."

"Then read it to me over the phone and leave out the really dirty words," said Don.

"Okay, I can do that," the judge conceded.

Da da, da da, da da, da da
Da da, da da, da da,
Da da, da da, da da, da da
Fucked up and far from home.

Don didn't learn a thing, but his participation in the contest had led to the offer of the UVic job. He remained hopeful that the teaching gig might be the springboard to even bigger opportunities, like becoming the poet laureate of Canada.

His latest poem needed a title. "I'll give it to Sal Vachon," he remarked to his cat. "I'll call it Boundless Faith. He'll appreciate that." The cat merely blinked, which Don took as approbation.

He took the elevator up to the Vachons'. There was no answer to his knock. Perhaps that was just as well; his last meeting with Sal had ended in a falling-out, although Don figured the argument had started innocently enough.

"Have you heard about the randy priest?" Don had asked Sal, accepting the latter's gracious invitation to come in for tea and cookies.

Figuring this was an anti-Catholic joke, Sal didn't mind hearing the answer, hoping it slagged the Pope.

"He was sinner qua nun. In the monastery he was constantly trying to get into the habit. When he did, he always waited for the second coming."

This was met with a stone-faced stare from Sal, so Don tried another one. "Have you heard about the nymphomaniacal Israelite?"

"No, I haven't." Sal's arms were crossed and his voice was chill.

"She was always trying to make a prophet!"

"Ten thousand comedians out of work and you're trying to be funny?" said Sal. The preacher told plenty of jokes in his sermons, but he didn't like it when others appeared to mock religion and question its teachings. Still, he had wondered how Noah could have fathered his first child at the age of five hundred, as stated in Genesis 5:32.

Don declared that he didn't subscribe to the cap the Jehovah's Witnesses placed on the number of people who could enter Heaven.

"The actual quote from the book of Revelation 14: 3-4 is: *144,000 living people who be deemed worthy of salvation during the final judgment, did not defile themselves with women, for they kept themselves pure.* So obviously, if you've had sex with a woman, you won't be saved. And women in general are excluded. What kind of cowyard confetti is that?" he asked Sal.

"Don't use that kind of language when you're referring to the holy writings in the Bible," Sal said angrily.

But Don pressed his point. "So none of the saved would be women, and certainly not lesbians.

"Furthermore, Sal, John, the alleged author of Revelation, was one tough hombre and his writings reveal the mind of a maniac – a God-skewed zealot who must have been on acid and should have been locked up and put on Prozac.

"Take a look at that whole bloody book of Revelation. It is, hands down, the most deranged section in the Bible. Like the Song of Songs, written by another superstar of the Bible, Solomon, it's an oddball book. You could also include Ecclesiastes in that category."

"You're a heretic," Sal exploded, "and I don't have to listen to this shit. I'm convinced that you will never get to Heaven."

"I wouldn't want to," Don replied. "The only place in the Bible in which Heaven is described is in Revelation, and it sounds like a terrifying place that only a madman could enjoy. Read your Bible, Sal, you're supposed to be the expert. John says, in Revelation 4:2-8, . . . *before me was a throne . . . and the One who sat there had the appearance of jasper . . . From the throne came flashes of lightning, rumblings and peals of thunder . . . Around the throne were four living creatures, and they were covered with eyes, in front and in back . . . Day and night they never stopped saying: Holy, holy, holy is the Lord God Almighty, who was, and is, and is to come!*"

Sal, his index finger upraised, thundered, "*The time is near, I am coming soon!* Jesus says that three times in the Bible's final chapter. Revelation 22:12-13. And that's when you'll get what's coming to you, Don, you blasphemous bastard. No sexually immoral poets will be allowed into Heaven."

"That was written two thousand years ago," Don pointed out. "How come he hasn't shown up yet?"

With that, Sal had unceremoniously ejected Don from his condo and slammed the door behind him.

But there was to be no such aggravated merriment today, much to Don's disappointment.

On his way back to his apartment, however, he ran into Phil Figgwiggin and another man, who were waiting for the elevator on the same floor.

Phil introduced Don to Mike Fowler and explained that

Mike was looking to purchase a condo in the same building.

Don seized the opportunity for a new audience. "Well then, it's only neighbourly of me to share my latest poem with you."

Ignoring Phil's frantic eyebrow signals, Mike accepted the proffered sheet and read.

"This one's hunky-dory," Mike commented tactfully. "But I hear from Phil that these are usually on the raunchy side. Are you cleaning up your act?"

"Not really," Don replied.

"I'm not saying you should," Mike hastened to add, "but what I think would do you a world of good would be a cherry float. Get some action instead of words."

"What's a cherry float?"

"A virgin on a waterbed!"

No Dance on the Mattress

O rder in the Court! The Honourable Mr. Justice Wade Aminette presiding," announced the Clerk of Court. The Judge entered Courtroom B of the downtown Victoria courthouse, where a small drama was about to be played out, the preliminary hearing in the case of *Crown v. Thistle Fielgud*. The panelled room was half-filled with interested parties and a few habitués seeking safe harbour from the rain outside.

Seated next to the Crown, in the person of Prosecutor Lee Gallotay, was Detective Constable Colin Allkarz, the original instigator of this legal contest.

Phil Figgwiggin immediately rose to his feet at the defence table to address the Court. "I wish to make application, Milord, for an Order of the Court quashing the charges against my client, Thistle Fielgud. I bring this application prior to the Crown's case so that you will bear it in mind during this preliminary hearing and thus be better able to assess its merits and come to a decision."

"On what grounds, Mr. Figgwiggin?"

"Lack of adequate or reasonable evidence that she has committed any of the crimes as charged. The prosecution's case is frivolous, without merit, and should be dismissed summarily. This honest working girl does not deserve a criminal record."

Lee Gallotay leaped up from his chair in feigned outrage. "Really Milord, I must strenuously object!" he said, much too strenuously.

Justice Aminette paused for a moment. He knew that Figgwiggin usually had a reasonable legal point to make. Wade was an optimist, like the man who always went on fishing trips with a camera and a frying pan. *If I drop a quarter in this collection plate I'll get a five-dollar sermon, but what the hey, why not hear what he has to say, even if it is only that the butler did it.* "Objection overruled."

"The deceased was preparing to have intimate sexual relations with my client at his request," Phil explained. "She was only deciding whether to comply when Fitzhugh dropped dead from over-excitement. My client did nothing, but if she *were* to do something, it would be to bring a suit for malicious prosecution. This is an abuse of due legal process and these charges should be quashed."

Justice Aminette took a long look at Thistle, seated primly next to her counsel. Despite the conservative note struck by her navy suit and white blouse, Aminette thought, It's a wonder they didn't charge her with carrying concealed weapons of mass excitement. That is a dangerous set of gazoopies she has there. No wonder Fitzhugh wanted to beanbag her.

Referring to his case file, the justice said, "So the deceased, Luke Howard Fitzhugh, was the screwor and your client was the potential screwee. Were they found in the alltogether, as it were?"

"No, Milord. Technically, she was in her working clothes. But she now admits that she was in the deceased's room, whereas previously she had told the police that she was not. She made that statement because she'd been frightened spitless by her interrogators and the predicament in which she found herself. Although she has been charged with obstruction of justice in that regard, it is my contention and submission that, under the circumstances, her actions were reasonable and that this charge should be dismissed.

"We will show that the tactics of the police were utterly deplorable, demonstrating a clear, calculated and egregious course of conduct intended to deprive Miss Fielgud of her Charter rights and her rights under common law. That is in addition to her right to have a lawyer present at her interrogation.

"Further, it is my considered opinion that the Crown only brings the charge of manslaughter in the second degree in order to persuade her to plead guilty to the lesser charge of obstruction. This, I submit, is unreasonable, and justice will not be served by pursuing either charge. 'The reasonable person adapts to the world,' as George Bernard Shaw said, 'while the unreasonable person persists in trying to adapt the world to himself. Therefore, all progress depends on unreasonable persons.' So I presume Your Lordship will take the doctrine of the reasonable man into consideration when coming to a decision."

"Certainly, Mr. Figgwiggin. I'll hear from the Crown on these charges in a moment, but what, Mr. Figgwiggin, is your version of the evidence relating to the death of Luke Howard Fitzhugh?"

"He invited my client to his room, intending to take advantage of what he hoped would be her sexual generosity. He had a heart condition of which he may or may not have been aware. He had been drinking, heavily. He took a substance called Spanish fly in order to enhance his hoped-for performance, the quality of which he may have doubted, and to increase his pleasure. Those were his own decisions, not those of my client. The contention of the Crown that she somehow fornicated him to death is ridiculous in the extreme."

"Why?" asked the justice, glancing at Thistle. *Might be a pleasant way to cash in one's chips.*

"Because, Milord, to put it in the vernacular, there was no dance on the mattress, she did not haul his ashes, there was no leg-over and he did not hide the salami, lay any pipe, plough the back forty or score between the posts."

"No need to continue in that vein, Mr. Figgwiggin, I get your drift. I'd hate to think that you were showing disrespect to the Court. I take it you're stating that no intercourse took place."

"Correct, Milord."

"All right, I will take cognizance of your application at the end of the prelim. Mr. Gallotay, do you have anything to add in this regard?"

Gallotay stood and declared, "Yes, Milord, I certainly have. The accused is responsible for the death of Fitzhugh, she facilitated the crime and therefore is indirectly guilty of manslaughter."

Phil got to his feet again. "My learned friend refers to a crime. Where is the crime here? Fitzhugh is responsible for his own demise by resigning from the human race and actually cheating the cardiologists out of a job. As the man said when an accordion was thrown from an upper-storey window and landed on his head, *res ipsa loquitur.* For the benefit of the spectators who are not familiar with Latin, that means that the facts speak for themselves."

"I've heard enough on the subject at this point. You may proceed for the Crown, Mr. Gallotay."

The prosecutor called his first witness, Dawn Gothere, an old harridan on the point of retirement from managing the Dominion Hotel. Gallotay approached her, a rapport-building smile on his face, and made the mistake of asking, "Mrs. Gothere, do you know me?"

She responded, "Why yes, Mr. Gallotay. I've known you since you were a young boy. Frankly, you're a big disappointment to me. You lie, you cheat on your wife, you manipulate people and talk about them behind their backs. You think you're a bigshot, but you haven't the brains to realize you'll never amount to anything more than a two-bit paper-pusher."

Gallotay was banjaxed but recovered quickly. He pointed across the courtroom and asked, "Mrs. Gothere, do you know the defence counsel?"

"I've known Mr. Figgwiggin since he was a youngster, too. He's lazy and bigoted and he has a drinking problem. He can't build a normal relationship with anyone and his law practice is a disgrace. Not to mention he cheated on his ex-wife with three different women. One of them was your wife, by the way."

Shaking his head, Phil rose to his feet. "Thank you, Dawn, for those kind words. I always liked you, too."

Judge Aminette asked both lawyers to approach the bench. In a quiet voice, he said, "If either of you idiots asks her if she knows me, I'll see that neither of you ever practises law again in this province! Now, get on with the case."

A visibly shaken Gallotay did so with alacrity, but not a great deal of confidence in his cause. He presented his evidence as if it bore a Made in Berzerkistan label. Inwardly, he was regretting that he had lent a receptive ear to Colin "Nail 'em and jail 'em" Allkarz.

Gallotay put Allkarz on the stand. The officer described his interrogation of Thistle at the police station, during which she stated that she had knocked on the deceased's hotel room door, but there was no answer. She had admitted she was an escort who charged up to a thousand dollars per date, but insisted she had not been in Fitzhugh's room. Only a hundred dollars had been found in Fitzhugh's wallet and he wouldn't have called her to his room if he couldn't pay for her services. QED, he must have been carrying a large sum of money, which was missing.

Forensic investigators had matched hairs on Fitzhugh's bed with samples taken from Fielgud at the station. This had taken considerable lab work, in addition to the time and effort expended by the police. As a result, Thistle's lies constituted obstruction of justice.

The conclusion to be derived from this, Gallotay maintained, was that Fielgud, a known high-priced call girl, had administered the liquor and drugs that had killed Luke Howard Fitzhugh, and that her motive was money. Her actions in this regard warranted the manslaughter charge.

Justice Aminette interrupted the proceedings, addressing both Gallotay and Figgwiggin, "Do you think we can
finish with this witness before lunch?" Neither lawyer
thought so.

"Then we'd better break."

The proceedings resumed at two, at which time Figgwiggin began the cross-examination of Colin Allkarz.

"I put it to you, Detective Constable, that you are a bully
and a braggart."

Colin turned to the judge. "He's attacking me. Do I have
to answer?"

"Yes," ruled Aminette.

Allkarz turned back to face Figgwiggin. "You didn't ask
me a question; you made a statement."

"All right, let me rephrase," said Figgwiggin. "Are you
a bully and a braggart?"

"No, I'm not."

"Then why did you act in that manner when my client
and I had a conference with you in your office?"

"How's that?"

"You said, and I paraphrase, 'Miss Fielgud must be guilty
of something and I'm going to make sure she's charged with
whatever is in the Code.' You implied that you were going
to throw the book at her. Then you rattled off several possible charges off the top of your head and stated, 'How do
you like them apples? And that may be just for starters.'"

"I wasn't taking notes," Colin objected.

"I was," Phil replied. "I told you then, and I'm repeating
it to you now, sir, that you're on a fishing expedition and
have no way to make such charges stick. And that's why I
maintain that you're a bully and a braggart, only looking for
convictions at my client's expense."

"And I'll bet the expense is plenty," Colin blurted angrily, "unless you're taking it out in trade."

Aminette leaned over the bench and glared at the cop.
"You're veering dangerously close to contempt of court, Detective Constable. It's my duty to protect learned counsel.

Now, answer his questions and don't be a smart-mouth."

"I'd like to make some pertinent observations in that regard, Milord, if I may," said Figgwiggin.

"Proceed."

"Social psychologists maintain that many of the problems that plague our society, from lying politicians to mistaken policemen, originate with the fact that humans simply cannot admit when they are wrong. We all form opinions about something – let's say about who committed a crime, as in this case – and then systematically reject or explain away any incoming evidence that contradicts our preferred thesis.

"I submit that in this case, the police believe they're being rational and scientific, but, in fact they're subconsciously falling prey to mental defence mechanisms that protect them from cognitive dissonance. Becoming team players is, to them, sometimes more important than admitting they're wrong and dropping charges they can't back up and which don't make any sense. Fortunately, however, the checks and balances of the justice system ensure that weak cases get weeded out. I respectfully submit that this is a textbook example in that regard."

"Thank you, Mr. Figgwiggin."

It took all day, but the hearing finally came to a close and His Lordship, not a judge to beat about the bush, presented his decision.

"Gentlemen, you have conducted your arguments with great ability, bringing out legal points of considerable importance and complexity." *My sweet Fanny Adams, the applesauce you have to include in summing up is really too much.*

"I have considered extensive arguments from both parties. It is fundamental to the rule of law that citizens before the bar receive justice – in other words, fair treatment. There is the old legal doctrine of the reasonable man, which Mr. Figgwiggin raised earlier. What, I asked myself, would a reasonable man have done under the circumstances in which the accused found herself on the fateful day of Luke Howard Fitzhugh's death? In my own research into the law, I found no reference to a reasonable woman, whereas one would have expected at least some passing mention of a reasonable person of the female gender. Therefore, and heretofore, I found that in common law, a 'reasonable woman' does not exist.

"In this case, I'm going to establish a precedent and state that the law, and therefore justice, should also apply to a reasonable woman. I realize that this ruling will irk many male chauvinists, but there is no precedent for anything until it's done for the first time; and there is precedent for that statement.

"I take cognizance of your application, Mr. Figgwiggin, and rule that the only charge that Miss Fielgud now still faces is that of obstruction; on the merit of which I will make no comment at this hearing, as that will have to be decided by the trial judge. All other charges against her are dismissed. You gentlemen are to consult the Clerk of the Court in order to set a trial date. Now, as to bail, what have you to say?"

Phil was on his feet immediately. "Milord, Thistle Fielgud is innocent until proven guilty. I'm asking that she be released on her own recognizance."

The prosecution begged to differ. "What's to stop her from skipping to points east, like Montreal or some other such sin city? We suggest $10,000 as a reasonable figure."

"I think you mean unreasonable, Mr. Gallotay," said Judge Wade Aminettee, "I believe two thousand is the figure you were looking for."

"I'll go surety for that," Phil volunteered.

"Done," said Aminette, peering at his wristwatch. He grimaced when he realized he wouldn't have time to play nine holes of golf before dusk. "Unless you have anything further to add, gentlemen, I will now close the court."

The following morning, the judge did get his round of golf in. His playing partner was a female pro he'd had his eye on for some time. His flirtation got him exactly nowhere, and he had to declare her an unpliable lay.

La Merde Frappe le Pan

Neale Downe placed another call to his RCMP source. "I heard about that boatload of pot your guys snatched."

"Yeah, whole lotta crowing going on around here," the voice replied.

"Any idea where they were headed with it, or who the prospective buyer was?"

"Nope."

"Might be nice to know their names. From what the papers say, the crew took a powder and you didn't manage to nail them."

"You got that right."

"Names?"

"The captain was Obadiah Hawke and his mate was a guy named Spokey Wheeler. We've stopped looking quite so hard for them. After all, we did seize the pot. Good thing, too, because the kudos we got for that won't mean much when word gets out about the pot somebody else stole from us."

"Really? What's that all about?" Neale asked.

"One of our trucks was hijacked on the incinerator run up by Duncan. What do you make of that?"

"I heard about it, but I've got nothing to say," Neale replied.

"I thought that's what you might say."

"'Nuff said, right? Those names may come in handy, though, so thanks. Bet I'll have more luck finding them than you did."

"Hope so. Good luck."

"La merde has just frapped le fan," said Inspector Acorn, not one to horse around. A thought entered his mind that applied to the current situation: If you give a man a fish you can feed him for a day, but if you teach a man to fish he can sit in the boat all day and get drunk.

Acorn was lecturing Constables Kerr and Potts in his office at Mountie headquarters in Victoria. "This heist has got to be solved, or your arses are in a sling. I'm trying to make up my mind what to do with you. Maybe I'll put you two on the cart-napping squad down at Save-On-Foods in Shit City. You're an embarrassment to the Force!"

John quaked inwardly as he absorbed Acorn's blistering criticism. He was beginning to think he was in the wrong business. But where could he get another job? Maybe he could run amok for a mucking company. Or maybe work as a cabin boy on a Greek vaseline tanker No, not that! His mind was reeling.

Their boss continued to berate them as the two deputy do-rights stood at attention before the Inspector. "We just made the biggest marijuana bust in our local history, got great publicity for it, and you two let some gang of stick-up artists steal nearly half a million bucks worth of prime BC pot that you were supposed to be guarding. You've made the Force a laughingstock in the War on Drugs. So we're going to go over it one more time. Did you get the licence plate number of the van those SOBs were using?"

"No, we didn't," said John, hanging his head. "We had to stop," he explained. "They were blocking the road."

"Two women, you say," Acorn put in. "And I'll bet these

weren't bag ladies, were they? Drop-dead babes in the woods, I'll wager. And maybe you thought you could score. Right?"

"The thought might have crossed our minds, sir," Joe admitted. "They were lookers, all right."

"And did that influence your decision to stop?"

"Maybe," said John. "But I was driving and I couldn't just run over the redhead. She was right in the middle of the left-hand lane between the van and, well, there wasn't much of a ditch. I stopped well back and as we said, Joe went out to investigate."

"Didn't you consider that it might be a trap?"

"Well, no, sir. Who would think of robbing an RCMP vehicle?"

"That's exactly the question, you morons. Who?"

Joe spoke up. "I may have a partial answer to that, sir, but I didn't want to bring it up until we'd gone over the whole story."

"Didn't realize you had a clue, Kerr. Okay, what is it?"

"It's a delicate matter, sir. A strange and shocking piece of information."

"I don't give a rat's ass if it's the Sale of Two Titties by Darles Chickens, or the Screwing of the Tern. Come on, let's hear it."

"In the fight," Joe blurted, "I ripped the mask off the guy who came out of the bushes at me."

"And . . . " Acorn prompted

"I recognized him."

"Well, why didn't you say so!?" Acorn exploded.

"I'm saying it now, sir."

Acorn calmed down. "Okay, good work, Constable. Maybe we're ungefucked."

"Maybe not, sir."

"Why not?"

"Because he was a Mountie!"

A sudden silence fell over the room as Acorn and Potts looked at one another in shock.

"What!? Are you sure? You're talking about a rogue officer, an inside job. Jesus H. European Christ! Who is it?"

"He's fairly new, transferred from the Interior a few months ago. Constable Stan Downe."

Neale and Gas dropped the girls off at Ready's place and continued on their way to the Canoe Brew Club and Marina on the Inner Harbour. It was now close to eleven, too early for the sodden traffic to start leaving this particular pissetorium, and hence relatively quiet.

They parked as close as possible to the water, where a goodly (and some badly) number of boats were moored. Gaston had arranged with a small sloop owner to store the loot for what he hoped would only be a short period of time.

Rowan Debotte was singing in the galley of *The Passing Wind* as he cooked up his favourite late-night lunch, an easily prepared something he called the Holey Cackleberry: Heat the frying pan, pour in some canola oil, cut a square hole in a piece of bread and let it start to fry with the loose bits on the side. Turn the bread before it browns too much, then drop an egg into the hole. Add salt and pepper and continue frying until the consistency of the egg pleases your fancy. Slap it on a plate and add some ketchup and open a bottle of beer.

Debotte had a mobile face that he always took with him wherever he went, and he loved to sing. Which wasn't to say that others liked to listen. He crooned a sailor's song in a ticky-tacky, schlocky voice:

As I walked one evening upon my night's career,
I spied a pretty fine ship, and to her I did steer,
I hoisted up my signal that she did quickly view,
And when I had my bunting up, she immediately hove to.
She had a dark and roving eye, and her hair hung down
in ringlets,

A nice girl, a decent girl, but one of the rakish kind.

"Excuse me, sir," she said to me, "for being out so late,
"For if my parents knew of this, then sad would be my
fate."
"My father is a minister – a good and virtuous man,
"My mother is a Methodist – I do the best I can."

I eyed that girl both up and down, for I'd heard. . .

Rowan was halfway through the song and his snack and
had stopped to pour more beer, when there was a knock on
the hull of the boat. "Who goes there?" he asked. "Friend
or foe?"
"Friend."
"Climb aboard then, friend."
Neale and Gas obliged, with Neale suggesting they im-
mediately unload their unspecified cargo onto *The Passing
Wind.*
While this operation was in progress, Neale asked Ro-
wan, "Do you think you could locate a couple of guys who
are making themselves hard to find at the moment?"
"These guys have names, I presume," said Rowan.
"Yeah, Obadiah 'Tommy' Hawke and Spokey Wheeler.
Originally from the Port Hardy area. We'd like to talk to
them."
"Why?"
"A business proposition," Gaston interrupted. "We'd
pay you if you can find them and arrange a meeting."
"What's it worth?" asked Rowan, a keen student of the
buck.
"Couple of C notes, maybe," Gas offered.
"I'll see what I can do," said Rowan, who figured he
could work this street for double the figure. Debotte had
grown up in the Port Hardy area. Tommy and the Spoke
were well known there. News traveled fast through Rowan's grapevine.

Dun Dit Dat, More to Dun Do

Rowan placed a call to an old school pal named Howie Duinn in Port Hardy. Duinn liked to exchange pleasantries before getting down to business, sort of a male bonding thing.

"How's it hanging, old timer?" Rowan asked.

"Rowan! You really want to know?"

"Of course."

"I'd complain, but how long would you listen?"

"No, I mean it, how ya keepin'?"

"I think the dry cleaners are shrinking the waistband on my pants and I'm getting less for my money each time I get a haircut. How about you?'

"I'm still trying to get ahead, but I'm just breakin' even. Livin' the life of Riley, though."

"Really? Does Riley know? Heard any good ones lately, Rowan?"

"See if this rings a bell. A man goes in for a thorough physical exam. He comes back a week later for the test results and says, 'Well, what's the story, Doctor? Am I healthy?'

"'Well,' says the doctor, 'I have some good news and some bad news.'

"The man says, 'Give me the bad news first.'

"'All right,' says the doctor. 'You have a fatal disease and you only have about a week to live.'

"'Oh, no!' says the man. 'But tell me, Doc, what's the good news?'

"The doctor asks him, 'You saw that great-looking receptionist out there?'

"The man says, 'Yes.'

"'Well,' says the doctor, 'I finally screwed her.'"

Howie laughed. "Good one. Okay. A man's on an airplane when the stewardess comes up to him and asks, 'Would you like some TWA soda, some TWA coffee, or some TWA milk?'

"The man looks at her and says, 'I want some TWA tea.' But enough of the jokes, I haven't heard from you for a while, so you must have a reason for calling, you old heller."

"Yeah, there's a reason. Where would I find Captain Tommy Hawke and that mate of his, that guy with the funny way of talking, Spokey Wheeler?"

"They aren't around these parts at the moment, or I would've heard."

"So where would they hang out if they were in the Lower Mainland area?"

"Where do you find the most fish?" asked Howie.

"Ah, lemme think. . ."

"Between the head and the tail, dummy. These are guys who never stray far from water. You could try along the Fraser River, maybe at one of those boat repair places. If they go into Vancouver, you'll find them around Main and Hastings in one of those old rooming hotels that seamen use. Chinatown's close by, and that's another possibility."

"How about here in Victoria?"

"Not their style, Rowan. Too high hat. Those two are basically shit-kickers, offensive in all categories, including nose hairs."

"If you hear anything, call me back, okay? You still got my number?"

"Sure. I'll call you – later than you may think, but sooner than you may expect."

"Roger. Have you heard this one? What's Irish and stays out all night?"

"What?"

"Paddy O'Furniture. Gotta go, Howie."

"Hold it, hold it! That was pretty clean, but I've got one for you. What do you get when you cross a rooster with an owl?"

"I'll bite."

"A cock that stays up all night!"

"Yeah, right." Rowan, not about to be outjoked, came up with: "What do you get when you cross a donkey with an onion?"

"Tell me."

"A piece of ass that brings tears to your eyes!"

"Enough already," said Howie. "I give up."

"Over and out, then."

Rowan poured himself a cup of coffee and went up on the deck of his motorized sloop. He plunked himself into the deck chair and thought about who else he could contact for information, all the while singing softly to himself:

> For he knew the world was round, oh,
> And tail oh, could be found, oh
> That smilin', smirkin', penis jerkin'
> Son-of-a-bitch, Columbo.

Meanwhile, back at the ranch, Horsemen in high places were discussing the honour of the RCMP and what to do about the dirty work at the crossroads involving that treacherous Constable Stan Downe and the disgruntling news that he was one of the scumbags who had harvested the Mountie grass.

"How can we sweep this mess under the rug?" asked Detective Sergeant Noah Whey.

"Can't. Won't," Rocky Acorn answered. "Even if we could,

do we want this bar steward in our midst, giving us the shaft? He is persona non grata. He's bent, a disgrace, a crook, and we don't want to be stuck with him."

"We could give him a fast shuffle up to Igloo City and nobody'd be the wiser."

"We'd know. Potts and Kerr would know, and who knows who else would get to know. Which isn't really the point, now, is it?"

"But think of the reputation of the Force."

Acorn was emphatic. "I am. And that's why he's going to be charged and stand trial for this crime."

"All right, I concur," said Whey, reluctantly. "Downe still doesn't know he's been found out, so let's charge him, pick him up and throw him in the slammer pronto."

"Right. Then interrogate him, see if he'll give up his accomplices."

"There has to be some mistake, fellas," Stan Downe insisted as he sat across the table from his interrogators. "I didn't do it, so help me Hannah."

One of his two questioners, Inspector Dick Tater, leaned most of his beefy frame into Downe's personal space. "The officers you robbed recognized you, so stop denying it."

"They're mistaken or they're lying. What did I ever do to them that they'd do this to me?"

"That's just it. They don't have it in for you, Stan. They don't dislike you. They just positively identified you as one of the heist artists. Speaking of which, who are the others?"

"How do I know? I wasn't there. I didn't do it, I keep telling you."

"Two broads and another guy. Come on, Stan, you cooperate and it might go a lot easier on you. Maybe you can make a deal. You're screwed, booed and tattooed right now, anyway."

"How can I do that? I don't know who the hell they are."

"We got a job to do, you know that. We're not going to

play good cop, bad cop with you, Stan, or slap you silly. But
do yourself a favour, man, stop fiddlefarting around and
give us a confession."

"I've already confessed to you. Listen carefully, I'm going to tell you this only once more. I didn't do it!"

"I gotta say, it was a slick plan. Too bad it didn't work.
But we've had enough of your bullshit. Do you want your
one phone call?"

"Yeah, I do. You know, I never did like our motto, the
Mounties always get their man. It'd be far healthier if they
got a girl. Okay, if you're not prepared to believe me, I want
a lawyer. Gimme the phone."

Stan dialed Phil Figgwiggin.

And where was Phil? With his new pal Mike Fowler, in-
specting the Fowlers' new condo, debating what renovations
should be carried out before Mike and Evelyn brought in
the rest of their goods.

"Am I going to miss life on Hornby?" mused Mike. "Had
lots of memorable experiences there."

"It's a great place, no question. But I'm sure you'll find
other things to do here," Phil commiserated.

"No doubt," said Mike, "but right now I've got mixed
emotions."

"Sorta like watching your mother-in-law drive over a
cliff in your new Cadillac?"

"That's about it," said Mike, smiling. "Did I ever tell you
about that mare named Old Bess?"

"No, you didn't," said Phil.

"Had a backbone that could slice a rider in two. If it was
too cold, she'd lie down and refuse to get up. Then Evelyn
would give her a shot of Dr. Bell's Miracle Wonder Drug for
Horses, which fired her off the ground like a rocket. There
was an old well by one of the barns that had been filled in,
and in the winter, heavy rains made the soil around the well
really soft. My two kids were riding Bess and another horse
one day and the old mare stepped onto a soft spot and sank.

"The soil was like quicksand and Bess got so bogged down, only her head and front legs were free. JoAnn rode back to the house and yelled for help. Evelyn called me, then started making phone calls to the neighbours. JoAnn rode around to several houses around us. Soon a group of over-excited men turned up at Seabreeze, talking chains, pulleys and ropes.

"Evelyn grabbed the Dr. Bell's Wonder Drug and got one of the guys, Sid Slate, to calm down enough to listen to her. By this time, Bess was looking near death. To humour Evelyn, Sid gave Bess a shot of the medicine and stood back. That ancient mare rose up out of the muck like she was jet-propelled, and almost leaped over Sid, who'd given her a double dose. Sid, pale as a ghost, asked Evelyn what in blazes was in that stuff, because he could sure use some of it himself. The story got around, and the women on Hornby Island were all set to use it on their husbands, until a doctor warned them that one drop could kill a person.

"I'd look out the window," Mike continued, "and that crazy horse would be lying on the ground, I'm damned sure on purpose, and we'd rush out and give her a shot of Dr. Bell's."

"Have you got any of that stuff with you?" asked Phil, "I'm willing to take a chance on it right now."

"No, but we could be seen to go down to the Bengal Room at the Empress Hotel and try a few shots of them there what-are-theys."

"You're on, Mike."

Jesus is Watching You

Sal Vachon said to Doggerel Don, "The Bible never reveals what kind of forbidden fruit Adam and Eve ate. Why people persist in saying it was an apple is a mystery. We in the Seventh Day Absentist Church believe it was a banana.

"Is that the only difference between your outfit and the rest of the apple proponents?" asked Don.

They had bumped into each other in the laundry room of the Whynan Beach Road complex and seamlessly resumed their customary debate about religion.

"We speak in tongues more often than the others."

"Is that so? When outsiders show up at your meetings they'll think you're out of your collective minds." Don threw his dirty laundry into the machine.

"Look, you asked me, I'm telling you! We believe baptism should be performed using the blood of an ox, the way Moses first did it, as stated in Exodus 24:5-8. But I'll admit this has become rather difficult. Another rule we adopt in our church – no altar to God should have steps."

"Why on Earth would that be?"

"That was God's instruction to Moses. You can read it

in Exodus 20:26. People ascending steps might expose their genitals!"

"God forbid."

"God even told Moses that Aaron and his sons must always wear underwear when they enter God's tent or else they'll be killed. That's in Exodus 28:42-43, so you see–"

"What I see," Don interrupted, "is that God seems to have an avid interest in human genitals. What's up with that? Speaking of genitals, what's your position on circumcision?"

"It's true that God made a covenant with Abraham and demanded that he – and all of his descendents – seal the deal by being circumcised. That's in Genesis 17:10."

"Why didn't God ever explain why slicing away the foreskin was so important? It seems peculiar, given the Bible's tirades against exposing the genitals. What good is a distinguishing self-mutilation that no one's allowed to see?"

"There are practical health applications," Sal said, unable to come up with anything better.

"Now, yeah. But then? I did read, though, in Genesis 34, that the Prince of Shechem raped Jacob's daughter, then fell in love with her and wanted to marry her. Jacob's sons said the wedding would only happen if the prince and every man in his city were circumcised. The prince agreed, though why in hell the other men would, I can't imagine. While he and his male citizens were still recovering from these painful dick operations, Jacob's sons attacked the city, plundering and pillaging, enslaving the women and killing all the men."

"Don't get smart with me, Don."

"Sal, Sal, I'm just asking questions out of a desire to know the Bible a bit better. Don't take it personally. You've got to admit, that was one smart example of military strategy. Might even get incorporated into US foreign policy."

"Well, what else do you want to know, you Bible-banging heretic?"

"Why do you guys palm off some of the sleaziest, trashiest people in the Bible as role models?"

"Like who?"

"Well, take Jacob and his family, for instance. Tell me if this isn't the true story. Jacob cheats Esau, his dumb twin brother, and brazenly lies to Isaac, his blind old father, so that he can become the chief heir to Isaac's property. That's grand larceny. Jacob wants to have sex with his lovely first cousin Rachel. That's incest. But her father demands seven years of labor in exchange. That's exploitation. Jacob does his time, then on the wedding night, Rachel's father, who's a con artist, tricks Jacob into having sex with Leah, Rachel's ugly sister. That's fraud. Then Rachel's father gladly gives Rachel to Jacob as a second wife in exchange for seven more years of labor. That's a swindle.

"You start to feel sorry for old Jacob at this point, but then things begin to improve for the schmuck. Rachel and Leah battle for his favor by giving him their maids as sex partners. That's living off the avails. Jacob becomes rich by cheating his father-in-law out of his best sheep and goats. That's embezzlement. Jacob then skips town with his booty and his women. That's absconding. He tells Rachel and Leah that his prosperity is an act of God. That's delusional perjury.

"Modern corporations and CEOs have been reading this story, from Genesis 30:31-34; 37-42; 31:4-5 and 8-9, ever since and using it as a blueprint.

"Judah, one of Jacob's sons, in Genesis 38:11-19, has sex with his daughter-in-law after she tricks him into thinking she's a prostitute. That's pimping.

"Joseph, another of Jacob's sons, declares that God has made him 'Lord of all Egypt' and refuses to give grain to its starving people unless they sell themselves into slavery to his master, who's the Pharaoh, not God. Genesis 45:9; 47:13-21. That's human slavery. Meanwhile, Onan is spilling his semen on the ground instead of impregnating his sister-in-law, which is what God wanted him to do, so God kills Onan – Genesis 38:1-10. That's murder.

"Wouldn't you say, Sal, that Jacob's family makes the Mafia look like saints?"

"How can you say such outrageous things, Don, you flaming atheist?" Sal was red-faced and breathing heavily.

"You mean secular humanist, Sal. First, because those tales are in the Bible. Second, because the Bible records a conspiracy theory, one of the oldest, most influential and controversial of all. The abbreviation for this theory is the code name GOD.

"There were several catastrophes in ancient history that triggered human sacrifice. The traumatized survivors of these senseless, gruesome and deadly destructive events, like earthquakes, floods and volcanic eruptions, tried to make some sense of them by inventing secret, almighty masterminds of the catastrophes – gods – who were punishing mankind with terror attacks from the heavens.

"In order to rid themselves of the horror and psychologically master the situation, the survivors re-enacted the catastrophes by staging bloody animal and human sacrifices. But no celestial body or earthly disaster can be influenced by offerings of virgins and sheep."

"Are you some kind of an asshole, or what?" asked an incredulous Sal, looking as if he might have a coronary.

"What?" answered Don.

"You heard me, you irreligious, hellacious, motor-mouth shit-disturber. Jesus is watching you, and you'll be punished for your blasphemy. Now get the hell out of here before I completely lose my self-control!"

With that, Sal began hurling wet clothes from his laundry basket, striking the rapidly retreating Don in the back of the head with a pair of oversize briefs.

Still chuckling as he stepped back inside his condo, Don put pen to paper:

JESUS SAVES

The night was still, there was no moon, the dark made him unseen,
And the burglar waited by the door, his senses all acute.

No sounds of human presence here, the job was to be
clean.

A craftsman who had planned his moves, he really was
astute.

A muffled click, the latch was done and up the stairs he
crept.

He swept the house with practiced eye till he was satisfied

That none but he was in that house and this he would
accept.

He reached out for the new TV and then he nearly died.

"JESUS IS WATCHING YOU!" he heard. The voice came
from the gloom.

He broke into an ice-cold sweat. Oh, where was he to
hide?

He stood stock-still, no further sound came from the
darkened room.

At last his racing heart slowed down, with breath returned his pride.

His courage back, he gave a shrug. It's not a thing to
fear!

So to the task at hand he moved, he reached again to
learn

"JESUS IS WATCHING YOU!" The voice rang in his
ear.

Fear clutched his throat, his heart stood still, his panic
made him turn.

Relief released his tortured soul, his darkened lamp re-
vealed

A little parrot on its stand. He could be jovial now.

"Are you the one that spoke just now?" he to the bird
appealed.

"I must say, you're a feisty one, but please don't let us
row."

"Yes, I'm the one that spoke to you and my master calls me Dear."

"What kind of man would call you Dear, or does he think it pleases?"

The parrot's words the thief took in with a paralyzing fear

"He's the kind of a man who also calls that vicious Doberman Jesus!"

Why Keep a Dog and Bark Yourself?

It took him a couple of days, but Rowan Debotte got a line on Tommy Hawke and Spokey Wheeler. He left a message for Gaston that he wanted to make contact. Gas and Neale showed up promptly at his sloop.

"How much did you say this information was worth?" was the first question Rowan asked.

"A couple of C notes, as I recall," Neale answered.

"It sure would be nice if you could sweeten the pot," said Rowan, "I had a few expenses myself in order to get the dope. No pun intended."

Gaston grunted. "Well, I'll be a dirty word. How sweet? We're not made of dough, you know."

"Yeah, but I'd accept maybe another C note to spill the beans on those boys. Now, to set up a meeting, well, that would maybe run up to five hundred. And cheap at that price, 'cause they're not anxious to talk to anybody. 'Course, I'm the guy who can assure them they won't detect the odor of federal horse manure when you show up."

Neale glared, then peeled off five hundreds and gave Rowan the money. "Okay, let's have it."

"Thanks." Rowan folded the notes and stuffed them into

the left breast pocket of his plaid shirt. "You're going to have to go to Vancouver. They want to meet at the Astoria Hotel on East Hastings. The Waldorf's farther down the street, but it doesn't have a beer parlour. They wanna be tossing back a few cool ones, with you pickin' up the tab. Name the time and I'll get back to them."

Phil picked up an urgent message from the Mountie slammer. A Constable Stanley Downe wanted to see him right away. Something about being held for a major theft and needing to talk to a lawyer asap. I know a Downe, but not Stanley, Phil thought.

"You interested in coming along?" he asked Mike Fowler, who'd stayed for lunch.

"Sure."

"You'd have to keep your mouth shut and just observe. Promise?"

"No problem."

At the police station, Phil grabbed the charge sheet, then he and Mike were ushered into a sparsely furnished, windowless room. A wooden counter ran across the width of the space, its surface divided by Plexiglas pierced with openings through which conversations could take place. The two visitors pulled up chairs in front of one location and waited.

After a few minutes an officer brought the prisoner through a door and seated him opposite Phil and Mike.

Phil's jaw dropped an inch, Mike's maybe two, but neither said anything for several seconds as they stared at the prisoner.

I'm looking at Neale Downe, thought Phil, holding his hand out for Mike to remain silent. Phil struggled for breath, but his legal training kicked in. "Have we met before?" he asked.

"No. I'm Constable Stanley Downe of the Royal Canadian Mounted Police."

"Your phone call mentioned theft, and that's the charge

I'm reading on this sheet. I take it a large quantity of marijuana is involved?"

"That's right."

"Shall we talk about it? In detail?"

"Not here."

"Why not, may I ask?"

"I work here. The place is probably bugged."

"Surely not. The law doesn't allow eavesdropping on conversations between counsel and client."

"Let me give you an example, so you get my drift. Have you ever been driving down the highway at exactly the speed limit, say a hundred kilometers an hour, and a couple of cop cars pass you doing ninety? A few minutes down the road, you find them setting up a speed trap."

"That could happen," Phil said, wondering what the point was.

"I'm just saying, sometimes the rules don't apply. And in this case, my superiors are so pissed off, they've decided not to do the usual ass-covering routine. They just might try bending the rules."

"Then where shall we talk?"

"You could apply for bail, but I'm not likely to get it. I've told them I'm innocent, but they're not listening."

"I haven't said I was going to represent you yet," Phil reminded him. "I don't usually ask so directly, since it might interfere with the best defence I could supply if I take on the case. But you've just said you're not guilty."

"Correct."

"I believe you. I'll take your case. Don't talk to anyone else; let me do that."

"Sounds good to me."

"I'll check whether bail is possible."

"As I said, I doubt it, but we can try. The Force sees this theft as treachery and they're determined to bust my balls."

"In that case, keep your pecker up, Stanley," Phil quipped. Indicating Mike, he added, "My assistant and I might as well go now. I'll talk to the prosecutor, ascertain their *prima facie* case, consider whether it's likely to prevail in court, and get back to you in due course."

"Thanks for coming down, Mr. Figgwiggin. I feel better now." Stan smiled for the first time during the interview.

Phil had a brief discussion with a Mountie officer, his manner cold, who said he would have the prosecutor get in touch with Phil regarding the details of the case against Downe.

In the car, Phil turned to Mike with a quizzical look.

"Doppleganger!" Mike burst out. "You want my opinion?"

"Certainly."

"We better find Neale Downe as soon as possible."

"My thoughts exactly," Phil said.

"Trouble is, he left Hornby without saying good-bye."

"The criminal standard of proof requires moral certainty and not mere likelihood. Maybe I can shift the burden of proof. But why they are charging Stan at all?"

"What do you mean?" asked Mike.

"The RCMP has a culture of covering up corrupt behavior and abuse of power. It seems more likely they'd just take the hit and forget about it. Send the bad apple, assuming he was guilty, to a remote posting."

"Right," Mike agreed. "Their motto isn't get your man, but cover your ass. Maybe they're using Downe to try to improve that image."

"I've talked to a former ethics adviser and representative of the rank and file in the Force's employee staff association. He maintained there was internal harassment on a broad scale. If you tried to stop it, you opened yourself up to retaliation."

"Well, it *is* a paramilitary outfit," Mike pointed out. "They're gonna protect the organization at any cost."

"They're supposed to have zero tolerance for unethical conduct. But maybe you're right, Mike. In this case they must be so pissed off, they've thrown all that out the window."

Ann Kerzaway, temporarily at loose ends since the pot caper up at Duncan, invited her new friend Helen to come over and try some of the stash of Mary Jane. Sitting on the sofa in Ann's condo, they rolled a couple of joints and lit up.

"Better than Acapulco Gold," Ann commented after a couple of hits.

"Yeah, BC shit beats the foreign stuff every time." Helen slid further down in her seat.

"But this is different, maybe we should give it a new name," Ann replied, attaching a roach clip to her cigarette. "It came from Port Hardy, so maybe something like Hardy High Grass."

"Nah, we can do better than that. These bods made the heist possible, so maybe Pussy Pot."

"That's a little better."

"I hope your guys finish their business soon and get the dough. Then maybe we can have a party. Maybe even a masquerade party. I sure love those."

"Haven't been to one in a long time myself," said Ann.

"One Halloween," Helen reminisced after taking a huge drag, "there was a party where we were supposed to dress up as emotions. So one guy came all dressed in green. You know, envy." Ann nodded languidly. "I wore all blue and everybody yelled, 'Sadness!'"

"Sounds like fun," said Ann, throwing her head back against the sofa.

"Late in the evening this guy shows up. No costume. He was stark naked and his dick was in a bowl of pudding. Nobody had a clue, so we asked him, What the hell emotion is that supposed to be?

"'Anger; I'm fuckin' dis custard!' the guy says." Both women collapsed in laughter.

Still giggling, Ann managed to say, "How about we walk down to that new pub on Government? You know, the one they made out of an old bank building. It's Irish, I think."

"Okay. A cold beer would go down well, maybe some munchies."

Ann and Helen grabbed the only free table in the Spotted Owl. The establishment had a minimum, and they spotted a waitress that was wearing it. The only thing holding up her dress was a city ordinance.

Two guys at the next table were trying but failing not to stare. A doctor would have had a hard time finding a place to give her an injection without having it show.

"Tough competition here," Helen said in disgust. The girls signalled for service, but the men naturally got the attention of the waitress first. They ordered a pair of Budweisers. The waitress shouted to the bar, "Two Buds!" She then turned to Ann and Helen. "What'll you ladies have?"

"Well," said Ann, "we were going to order Country Club, but we'll change that to India Pale Ale."

Helen gazed around the room, one elbow on the table, her chin in her hand. "I've got my eye on that Neale guy. He's a hunk. What do you figure are my chances?"

"Not good, Helen. Not right now, anyway."

"Why not?"

"Gas tells me he's in love with a gal called Florence Ealing. Met her when she was holidaying on Hornby Island. He lived there until recently. But I hear she disappeared and he's trying to find her. If he doesn't, then that's another ball game, where you could maybe hit a home run if you swung for the fences." Ann sat up straighter. "But hey, maybe I got just the guy for you. He lives in our building. Name of Don McGraw."

"What does he do?"

"Some kinda poet, and maybe that's a little geeky. Okay, he *is* geeky. And skinny. But I hear he's going to be a university professor."

Given the mixed review, Helen didn't seem impressed. "I guess I can give him the once-over."

"Okay, I'll set it up. You know how the quiet ones can sometimes surprise you. Maybe he's got the size and stamina you've always dreamed of." Their hoots and shrieks drew the roving eyes of the two at the next table, launching the women into even louder fits of laughter.

Dirty Dick's Filling Station

There are still bars in Canada where badasses congregate, safe from the intrusion of appleknockers, hayseeds or gobshites. The low-rent bar is their natural turf, strictly hostile territory, reminiscent of an older, rougher era. It is inhabited by prostitutes, thieves, workingmen, actors, musicians and the rest of the great unwashed; male and female veterans of military and matrimonial wars, wetting their whistles to forget battles fought and injuries sustained.

Neale and Gaston, who between them had probably seen too many Westerns, stood across the street from the Astoria Bar and Grill, aptly nicknamed Dirty Dick's Filling Station.

"Couple of things we gotta remember," said Gaston, hitching up his pants. "Don't eat the Happy Hour hot dogs. They've been there a long time and no regular touches them. Also, if there's a choice between a seat next to a hot-looking girl and one by some guys, pick the seat next to the guys. That sends a message that you're there to drink, not get laid."

"That's good advice," Neale replied. "Besides, she could have a boyfriend who's the possessive type. We don't want to stir up a nest of sexual jealousy. We go in with confidence, we get the information, we get out. We buy the drinks but Rowan pays these guys off, not us." At Gas's nod, Neale said, "Okay, let's go."

They stepped off the sidewalk just as a drunk with the blind staggers came through the boozery doors.

Neale and Gas stood still in the open doorway, the late afternoon light behind them, their expressions unreadable to those inside. The short pause allowed their eyes to adjust to the low light. They knew they were being watched and judged by angry eyes, guys who were looking for suckers and boobs to bilk. It was a dump, all right, a gloomy, smoky place, like the mess hall at Oakalla Prison.

They scoped the joint for potential adversaries, noting where they were sitting and what they were drinking. They weren't sure what Tommy Hawke and Spokey Wheeler looked like. Neale nodded at the bouncer, knowing he could be their best friend if things got ugly.

Neale slapped his hand down on the bar with enough force to be heard. The barkeep was busy pretending to polish glasses, likely a cover while he watered down the bottles of booze. When he made eye contact, Neale nodded slightly, then scanned the shelves to make sure he ordered a brand they carried. He didn't want to look like an idiot.

"Two shots of Canadian Club, straight up, water on the side," he ordered in a clear voice, then turned to face the room. Neale put his street-side elbow on the bar and the heel of his opposite foot on the bar rail and surveyed the scene. Gaston followed suit. The bartender slid coasters across the bar. Those two guys in the far corner, Neale said to himself. *Nobody else fits the picture.*

The rye arrived and, without turning, they listened as the bartender took their money to the till, made change and came back to hand it to them. Allowing several seconds to pass, they both turned and faced the drinks. They took simultaneous sips, rolling it over on their tongues to test the quality.

You don't sit down in a lion's den unless you know the lions. They took their drinks and walked over to the corner table.

"Am I talking to Captain Tommy Hawke?" asked Neale.

"We're waiting for someone," said Tommy. "Maybe you. Who sent you?"

"Rowan Debotte. And your friend would be Spokey Wheeler, right?"

"Right answer. Sit down." Hawke kicked a couple of chairs away from the table.

Neale signaled the scraggly waiter. "Two more of whatever these gentlemen are drinking." Turning back to Hawke, Neale remarked, "The *Chances R* was some great caper, too bad about the end result."

"Yeah, we were going to make a killing from that boatload, but it came a cropper, or should I say a copper."

"Hope you didn't come off too badly," Gaston commiserated.

Spoke spoke up. "We left no stern untoned to pull off that job and only made a small score. But now we don't give a phony buck. We have everything to seat our nudes, all sorts of farty acts." Gaston looked at Spokey in mild bewilderment.

"True enough," Tom agreed with the Spoke. "It's just that the Moundies are looking for us, 'cause they think they can prove we were on that boat."

"Let's suppose for a minute that you were," said Neale. "Where were you planning to unload the cargo?"

"That's what you want to know?" Tommy exchanged glances with Spoke.

"In a nutshell, yeah," Neale answered. "We want to talk to your contact, which should be no skin off your asses."

"True enough. So what's the deal?" asked Tom.

"You know the deal, Captain. Debotte's paying you, and we're buying your drinks for the evening and enough for you to buy a round for the house – which should make you popular here at Dirty Dick's." Neale slid a few bills across the table.

"Sounds okay to me," Spokey put in, reaching for the money. "It's a business doing pleasure with you guys. A turd in the hand is worth two in the bush. I mean a herd in the band is boo in the tush."

"What'd you say?" asked Gaston, scratching his head.

"I said a hand on the bush is worth two on the bird."

"He means we'll take it," Tommy translated. "The info won't be worth anything to us for a while and someone else may as well take advantage of it."

"Appreciate that."

Tom pulled a piece of paper from his jacket pocket. "Here it is. It's a boat and it can meet you. That was what was supposed to happen. The contact number's on the paper, including the password you should use. You have to be able to answer three riddles. If you don't give the exact answers, they hang up. That's it."

"Thanks," said Neale. "Now we're going to blow this joint. I'm getting the impression we're not welcome here."

The reason why was at the next table with some of his friends. A burly denizen of Dick's, who suddenly yelled, "What are you two ass bandit creampuffs doing here?"

"Matter of fact, here comes trouble now," said Neale, immediately rising and going to the heckler's table, his hands clenched at his sides.

Gaston got up behind him, thinking, Jeez, I hope this guy's a candyass playing tough for the crowd and not the real McCoy.

"How about another drink?" Neale asked evenly.

The ball was in the burly badass's court. Burly blew it bigtime, rejecting Neale's peacemaking offer. "Bugger off, shit-for-brains!" he said and started to get up.

Gas murmured, "Here they come, the nightly scum, their bloodshot eyes aflame."

Neale struck first, slamming the heel of his palm into the bridge of Burly's nose, then following through with an elbow to the jaw and a knee strike to the groin. Burly went down. And got up again. Neale finger-jabbed him in the esophagus, which quickly reorganized the bully's priorities. He collapsed again, groaning.

A deadly silence fell over Dirty Dick's. Neale turned back to Tommy's table and finished his drink. He wanted to stay cool; besides, he'd paid for the booze.

Two of Burly's friends threw back their chairs and rushed forward, only to be met by the watchful Gas. They didn't know dim mak or jujitsu. Using the momentum of the punch thrown by his first assailant, Gas flipped him into a somersault that landed the man in Tommy Hawke's lap. They both fell to the floor cursing, and a general donnybrook broke out. Gas ran the other guy into the wall.

"That guy's going to need a pyrocracktor," Spokey observed, ducking a punch and doing his best to weather the shitstorm. "This is going to be a fustercluck if I ever saw one."

Neale and Gaston headed for the door before Burly's other friends could decide whether the fight was over or not. Neale tossed a twenty to the bartender as he passed the bar. He took a last look at Burly, still trying to get up off the floor. He and Gas walked out onto East Hastings.

"Where'd you learn to fight like that?" Gas exclaimed. "You sure finished him off quick."

"I never liked fighting, but I watched my brother and remembered what he would have done. It was a jungle where we grew up. You learned to keep your cash in a money clip in your front pants pocket. If you drank, you knew your limits. If you didn't, you ran the risk of someone kicking the crap out of you when you were swacked.

"In a bar like Dirty Dick's, most fights are glorified pissing matches between drunken regulars. My brother Ted knew how to deal with a guy like that bozo back there. You use any means you can to win. Everything depends on staying in control, thinking fast and acting first. And that's what we're going to keep on doing."

The Last Blonde Joke

"We're going to have a small dinner party," Ann announced one evening after Gaston Ready had returned from Vancouver.

"Is that so?" answered Gas. "Who's invited?"

"I'm doing it for Helen, so she can meet Don McGraw, who'll be the fourth."

"Regular little matchmaker, aren't you? That knuckle-head owes me money."

"I know that, but he also needs a girlfriend."

"How do you know he wants one?"

"I know because he made me promise not to give you this eight hundred dollars until I got him a date," she lied as she handed over the dough.

"Well, I'll be damned," said an astonished Gas. He counted the bills, then said, "The little bastard paid off."

"Helen's available and she sure could use a steadying influence."

"You think Doggerel Don and those crazy poems he writes are a steadying influence?"

"Could be."

"At least we can be sure Helen's not a fowl of the law."

"Meaning what, exactly?"

"A stool pigeon."

"Of course not. She wouldn't tell anybody. Certainly not Don."

"Okay, let's do Don a favour. Helen looks good in anything she takes off. I'll buy some champagne."

Don was delighted to be invited, and turned up in his best bib and tucker, bearing flowers. Helen thought he was square but not unattractive, and surprisingly, an interesting conversationalist.

Ordinarily, Ann didn't butter her bread, because she didn't like to cook. She served nothing but leftovers, and Gaston could never remember the original meal. He'd eaten meals at home that he would have sent back in a restaurant. Tonight she had outdone herself, and Gaston salivated as he watched her prepare the gourmet spread she had purchased from Chef on the Run.

First, though, they irrigated their tonsils with the champagne, and the bubbly loosened up the party. After a few glasses of the panther piss, not stopping to consider whether the content would be popular, Don compulsively hauled out a new poem. He introduced it by saying he hoped it would be the last dumb blonde joke ever written. He dedicated this new work to the beautiful blonde Helen.

Oh, once in our fair city there was a pretty blonde,

She was fed up with dumb blonde jokes and decided to abscond.

So she dyed her sunny curls and to the country fled

She hoped with such a "head" start she'd nothing more to dread.

And so it was she loved the life, she couldn't get enough,

The birds, the beasts, the flowers and all that kind of stuff.

One day she went out walking and saw a flock of sheep.

She shouted to the shepherd, "How many do you keep?"

"How many would you say?

"If you can guess exactly, I'll give you one today.

"And you can pick the one you want, it's strictly up to you."

Our ex-blonde didn't hesitate: "There are four hundred and ninety-two."

"Amazing," said the shepherd, "You've won the right to choose."

With all the sheep to choose from, he'd nothing much to lose.

Again she didn't hesitate: "I'll take the black and white one.

"He's bigger than the other sheep and seems to have more fun."

The shepherd said, "Now fair is fair, it's now my turn to guess.

"Your choice of sheep has stumped me, and this I will confess,

"If I can tell your colour, before you dyed your hair,

"Will you give me back my sheepdog? I think that's only fair!"

Helen nearly fell off her chair laughing. This may not be catch and release; he could be a keeper, she said to herself.

Reading from the Book of Proverbs was like reading an endless list of Chinese fortune cookies – sayings that were strung together, one after another. Self-righteous Bible thumpers and religious rock star lyricists used these nuggets of ostensibly God-approved wisdom the world over.

Sal Vachon, who truly believed that God held the whole world in his hands, was no exception. He also believed Ecclesiastes 10:19, especially when passing the collection plate:

A feast is made for laughter and wine makes life merry, but money is the answer for everything.

Many well-dressed evangelicals gave their "mite" to Vachon to curry favour with God, since Vachon always told them, "When you give, it qualifies you to receive God's abundance. If you're not prospering, it's because you're not giving."

Even poor, frail old ladies would trot down his sawdust trail and put coins in the offering box of the church, as a quid pro quo for heavenly hopes and blessings.

Sal was preaching up a storm in Victoria on this sunny Sabbath, lauding to the heavens the beautiful nature of forgiveness as a way of life. "Is there anyone here in the congregation this morning who can stand up and say in all honesty that he has no enemies, that he has forgiven them all? Keep in mind that when you're done catching cod and go to meet your God, you'll want to be able to tell him you were a forgiving person."

No one rose and Sal continued, "Come now, good people, surely there must be some person who has forgiven all his enemies. Remember, forgiveness is the fragrance the violet sheds on the heel that has crushed it."

An old man in the back row of the church slowly and painfully rose to his feet and stood trembling before the worshippers.

"There now, my friends," Sal pontificated, "here we see a man who has done the righteous thing. Congratulations, sir. Can you tell the congregation how it came to pass that you forgave all your enemies?"

"It was easy," the man replied. "All the sons of bitches are dead."

After the sermon was finished and the collection taken, Sal shook hands with parishioners outside the church. One of them asked him, "Reverend, I'm having a lot of trouble with my wife. She's in a terrible mood, nagging me continually. I think she's suffering from pre-menstrual syndrome. What's the church's policy on PMS?"

Sal was nonplussed. He had never been asked that question before, and didn't know what stand the church had on the subject, if any. "I'll look it up in the Bible," he promised. "The Good Book contains the answer to everything."

The following week the parishioner was back and Sal told him that PMS was indeed mentioned in the Bible.

"Where?" inquired the astonished parishioner.

"Where it says: *and Mary rode Joseph's ass all the way into Jerusalem.*"

While his erstwhile helper, the Gas Man, was living it up, Neale was busy tending to business, phoning the number in the United States supplied by Hawke. He stated the password – turnip greens – which gave him access to the potential weed buyer. Then he had to solve three riddles to further establish that he was legit.

"Here's the first one, buddy," said the party at the other end of the line. "Three men are in a whorehouse. One man's hurrying up the stairs to one of the rooms, another guy's leaving the establishment, and the third is getting it on with one of the women. What's the nationality of each man?"

"Russian, Finnish and Himalayan," Neale read from his cheat sheet.

"Second: Why did the mother forbid her child to read Ivanhoe?"

"She heard it was full of Saxon violence."

"Here's the last one. Who are the three most constipated men in the Bible, and why?"

Neale read the answer. "Cain, because he wasn't Abel; Methuselah, who sat on the throne for nine hundred years; and Moses – God gave him two tablets and sent him into the wilderness."

"Okay, you got all three right. You're okay. Are we talking hard stuff?"

"No, soft."

"How much you got?"

"Just short of the amount you were expecting recently from

Port Hardy on the *Chances R*, captained by Tom Hawke."

"We could have done without that unlucky song and dance routine."

"You were prepared to pay $400,000. I'd go for the same deal, because what I've got is the same prime product. Better than Congo Bush, Durban Poison or Acapulco Gold. When you try some, you'll agree."

"We'll do that, all right. Name the location."

"Victoria."

"I'll send a man up there on the next plane. Give me the details on how he can contact you."

Neale crowed as he hung up the phone. Lady Luck was going to turn up trumps for him, as demand was high and US buyers were desperately short of supply.

Gordon Maymde, the front man for the buyers, was in Victoria faster than a buzzard on a rotting corpse. They needed pot now, were rolling in dough and willing to do a whip-around deal. Gordon was clued in to all the angles. The $400,000 Canadian would be held in trust by a tame Vancouver lawyer and released on proper transfer of the product. Neale Downe was going to use the same firm of legal eagles later on to launder the moolah offshore in the Cayman Islands.

As for the transfer itself, a yacht was set to dock in front of the Empress Hotel in Victoria's Inner Harbour within days.

Dewey Cheatem

Thistle Fielgud's second trial was now in progress with a slight change in personnel. This time the Honourable Mr. Justice Weldon Burger presided over the court, and prosecutor Lee Gallotay had been replaced by Dewey Cheatem.

Phil Figgwiggin, QC rose at the commencement to address the court. "Milord, this charge of obstruction against my client is, if I may say so, serious in name only, and in my humble opinion should have been dismissed along with the other charges at the preliminary hearing.

"The justice system is supposed to provide checks and balances to ensure weak cases get weeded out. The case before the court today is one that should get whacked. Astonishingly, police and prosecutors often refuse to admit they screwed up, even when slam-dunk evidence has proven them wrong.

"I shall primarily be asking that the case against Thistle Fielgud be dismissed on the ground that it is based purely upon circumstantial evidence. I will not bore you with a tiresome parade of case law in that regard, as you will already be aware of most of the content." Phil sat down.

Meaning that he hasn't bothered to look up any case law at all, thought a worried Justice Burger. *But from what I know about the case so far, I'm betting with myself that he has a winner here.*

Weldon was perturbed, and for good reason. He took another look at the accused, who sat demurely next to her counsel. *I'm not sure, but I think that's the call girl, all right. Damnation, I don't know if she recognizes me or not. We both had a skin-full as I remember it, at least I did. My arse must have been on backwards to get into a situation like that. My excuse? Seemed like a good idea at the time – the cause of all such shenanigans. But I can't say that I didn't have a good time. What am I going to do? Stop the trial right now and recuse myself? They'd ask me why. I damn sure couldn't tell them.*

The Crown had already launched into his opening statement and the trial was under way before Judge Burger had more time to think about how to solve his dilemma.

Dewey Cheatem was no chicken. He held his temper in check when mocked by younger colleagues, who were driven by the guiding principle of all prosecutors: if you can't say something bad about a person, don't say anything at all. Dewey was rumored to have been a busboy at the Last Supper. Whether he'd gotten any tips was another matter.

Cheatem's face bore a tired smile. He covered his prematurely bald pate with a bad hairpiece, matched only by his bad attitude. Dewey brought a few tough decades of experience to the case.

He began by playing the prostitute card for all it was worth, which might not be much. He'd been around the world in a rowboat and knew the difference between a cathouse and a courthouse – you got screwed in both places. He also knew the difference between a football game and a bawdy house – in football you kicked a punt.

As Dewey launched into a derogatory depiction of prostitution in general and call girls in particular, Figgwiggin rose to object vociferously, seizing on the opening Cheatem had just handed him to widen the scope of the trial.

"These remarks are not only offensive, but extraneous in a trial for obstruction of justice. But I must rise to the defence of prostitutes. They cannot organize a brothel where they can look out for one another and combine resources to buy medical care, security or insurance. What does the proscription against 'living off the avails' really mean? That a prostitute must work alone, shielded from the eyes of the law, unable to get bank credit or regularize her tax status or buy an RRSP if she wants one.

"What do the rules against 'communicating for the purpose of prostitution' mean? They mean that most hookers have to do business through the window of a car, which allows them mere seconds to size up their customer, or over the phone, which hardly lets them do so at all. However, Milord, my client is not on the street. We do admit, though, that she did misguidedly became a call girl."

And a damn good one, thought Weldon.

"She is also a victim in this case," Figgwiggin continued. "Johns have to bear their share of the responsibility for the sex trade, so it is ludicrous to blame the providers of a service that the johns want. Let's have no more of my learned friend's character assassination. My client merely hated poverty worse than sin, and should not therefore be tried and found wanton."

Justice Burger, sensing a way out, said, "I get your point, Counselor. What can it profit Canada to impose these strictures on prostitution? What social gain is there in keeping the trade out of sight, out of mind and on the run?"

Addressing the prosecution, Weldon said, "Your case is one of obstruction, Mr. Cheatem. Stick to it. Consider this your first and last warning to cease and desist in snide and derogatory remarks about hookers."

Phil was bemused, as it seemed the judge was buying into everything he was selling. Figgwiggin sank back into his chair and awaited the next development.

Allkarz took the stand and was sworn in. Cheatem conducted his examination-in-chief, bringing out testimony from the first trial where pertinent. He entered an audiotape of the interview between Allkarz and Fielgud into evidence and played it for the court. Dewey then turned to Phil and said, "Your Witness."

Phil rose to cross-examine. "During your interrogation of the accused, was she ever placed under oath?"

"No."

"Did she not appear voluntarily, at your request?"

"Yes."

"Was she represented by legal counsel?"

"She said she didn't need a lawyer."

"Did Miss Fielgud appear to be frightened during the interrogation?"

"Not frightened, but certainly nervous."

"Do you recall a subsequent interview with the accused when I was present?"

"Yes."

"Your attitude at that time was definitely threatening."

"I don't think so. My attitude remained the same throughout. I was trying to make sense of a crime scene."

"From that we can assume, your demeanour was the same at both interviews. Did you at any time tell or intimate to my client that she would be charged with a criminal offence relating to the death of Luke Howard Fitzhugh?"

"How would we know that until after the interrogation and before completing our investigation? She lied to us. Said she hadn't been in Fitzhugh's room."

"You mean the information could have helped. But how could it hurt?"

"Because it caused us a lot of extra work, and that constitutes obstruction."

"Put yourself in her shoes, Detective. Would you not likely have tried to distance yourself from the whole situation and deny any knowledge thereof?"

"I don't think I would have lied to the police."

"Wouldn't be the first time people have done so, now, would it?"

"No, it wouldn't – which usually means they have something to hide."

"You don't think perhaps she was just trying to protect herself from a police officer she thought was going to crack down on her, and didn't know what manner, shape or form that crackdown might take?"

"No comment."

"She finds herself in an unusual position. She knows she's done nothing wrong in regard to Fitzhugh's sudden death. What would you do in similar circumstances? Wouldn't you be inclined to tell the police you knew nothing about it?"

Colin turned to the Judge. "Do I have to answer that question, Milord?"

"No, you do not," said Burger.

"Then I will," said Phil. "I think many of us in the same circumstances would do the same thing. No more questions."

When it came time to present his defence, Phil decided not to put Thistle in the witness box, the place where most people go to perjure themselves, thus depriving Cheatem of a chance to pick holes in her testimony. In his summation, Phil stressed the lack of proof against his client.

Both sides having summed up, they awaited the court's decision.

Weldon Burger peered at Thistle. *It's not as if I'm not convinced of her innocence. Figgwiggin's arguments certainly have merit and would achieve the same result in any appeal court. But that's not going to happen. We're dealing with a biological urge here – the mysterious sex drive – and the law isn't going to do much good in solving it. Society has to change its attitudes about sex for money. How can one issue continue to plague generation after generation with no new plan for change? I don't blame this girl for clamming up with the police, she was frightened and wasn't under oath. So my decision won't be a big stretch, like my wife's mouth over a piano stool.* "Will the accused please rise while I pronounce judgment."

Thistle rose and faced the judge. She'd been watching
him throughout the trial and he certainly looked familiar,
but it was hard to tell in those robes. If she could see him in
the buff, she'd be sure. She gave him a big smile.
"I find the accused not guilty," Weldon declared.

They debated the best time to transfer the pot, and decided on broad daylight, in order to cause less suspicion.
Neale purloined a banner proclaiming the merits of Island
Produce and ran it around the base of the cabin of the *Passing Wind*. Rowan Debotte revved the engine, backed into the
Gorge Waterway, then turned and headed for Victoria's Inner Harbour.

With Neale and Gas aboard the sloop, they headed
across the bay toward a luxurious white yacht moored in
the marina along the cobbled embankment below the Empress Hotel. Running alongside, they unloaded the cargo
with the aid of the yacht's culinary staff. It turned out to be
a breeze, money for jam.

Everything's coming up aces, thought Neale. *All I have
to do is pay everyone off and then take the gravy train out of here.
Or a boat maybe – catch a petroleum tanker heading for the Virgin
Islands. Or how about Jamaica or somewhere in Mexico? But tell
me, where is fancy bred? In the heart or in the head? How begot,
how nourished and fed? I've got to find Florence Ealing and take
her with me. I can just see us now, lying on a sunny shore in Can-
cun, drinking cold Coronas.*

The dope drop completed, Rowan and Gas tootled back
to the Canoe & Brew Club marina. Neale decided to stroll
back down Government Street. He picked up a copy of the
Times-Communist at Munro Books, then sat on a bench in
the nearby square to peruse the news. A small item on page
three not only caught his eye, it jumped right off the page
into his suddenly bamboozled brain. *Local RCMP Officer Ar-
rested in Drug Heist*, screamed the headline.

*Constable Stanley Downe was charged yesterday with theft
in the recent highway hijacking of marijuana in the Duncan area.*

Police were reluctant to release further details due to security rea-
sons, but stated they were still seeking other members of a sus-
pected outlaw gang. Downe is being held without bail...

In shock, Neale stopped reading. He felt as if a big bird
with diarrhea had just crapped on his head. Jumping for joy
a moment earlier, now he was caught between a sweet dream
and a hard place. *How did this happen? What evidence could they
have on Stan? He's innocent. Well, only complicit. I can't take it on
the lam and let them cook his goose.*

"What I need is help," he said aloud. "And just maybe, I
know where to get it." A phone booth close by produced a
directory. He looked up the address. Phil Figgwiggin's office was only a few blocks away, in the CIBC bank building
on Douglas Street.

Crowne v. Downe

A mong those present on Stanley Downe's day in court was Doggerel Don McGraw, who made it a point to attend trials in which Figgwiggin was involved. Phil was Don's guru, someone who had never failed to defend the poor and the downtrodden whenever necessary.

Don sat in a back pew making notes in the scribbler he always carried. As he listened and observed the parade of cases prior to the one he'd come to see, he decided he'd try to compose a poem from the courtroom drama that would soon unfold before him.

Finally, the Clerk of the Court rose to announce the proceedings and read aloud the charges against Stan Downe.

Her Majesty the Queen v Stanley Downe
British Columbia Supreme Court Trial by Judge Alone
Mr. Justice Hugo Hoverdaire Presiding

Docket: 1166

Counsel:
Joseph Novark, QC for the Crown
Philip Figgwiggin, QC for the Accused
Subject: Sec. 334 Criminal Code

Everyone who commits theft is guilty of an indictable offence and liable to imprisonment for a term not exceeding ten years where the value of the property of anything that is stolen exceeds $5000.00; or is guilty of an offence punishable on summary conviction and liable to imprisonment for a term not exceeding two years where the value of what is stolen does not exceed $5000.00.

The prosecution had the first kick at the cat, to present its case based on all the provable facts at its disposal, in a fair and unbiased manner, starting, however, from the premise that those facts proved the guilt of the accused.

Joe Novark's colleagues often called him Joan. He hated being asked questions like, "Was Joan of Arc Noah's wife?" Tall, on the skinny side, it was hard to know what to make of him. Not unattractive, he was square-jawed, with shifty china-blue eyes and wavy blond hair. He looked like someone you might expect to find on the other side of a motel shower curtain, brandishing a knife.

The fact that his face bore a perpetual smile made the impression that much more disturbing, as if he were salivating over the many evildoers he was going to place behind bars. Joe was tense and nervous and figured every perp was guilty. He was also taciturn; he figured if he'd said something once, why say it again?

Novark began by outlining the circumstances and details of the robbery to the court, then continued with legal argument to bolster his case.

"The accused, Stanley Downe, committed the felony of theft, Milord, not theft of a few pennies, mind you, but theft of something worth hundreds of thousands of dollars, in a daylight robbery involving the use of force and bodily harm. He and his gang of three accomplices, the four thieves you might say, did this with malice aforethought.

"His motive was the usual one, simple and obvious – crass greed and the reward of a large financial coup, the same motivation of any bank robber. He had the knowledge of how, when and where the crime could be committed without much risk of failure. How else would the thieves have known where and when to strike if it had not been for the inside information he obtained from his employers?

"In short, he had the motive, means and opportunity to commit a robbery of this magnitude, for which he figured he would have little chance of getting caught. He was in the unique position, or so he thought, of being above suspicion. All he needed were some trusted accomplices. Not necessarily even ones of shady character, but possibly so – people who also sought an easy score. We don't know who these accomplices were, as Constable Downe refuses to name any of the other three perpetrators who were with him at the scene of the crime. Most likely they were people who are familiar with, or deal in, marijuana.

"This crime, no ordinary theft, but the theft of the nefarious drug of cannabis, is rendered particularly heinous because it was carried out by an officer of the law, a person sworn to carry on the war against drugs. This was breach of trust, no less, a dereliction of duty. Downe is a disgrace to his uniform and to the Department of Justice he has sworn to serve, all of which should be reflected in his sentence.

"The prosecution will place Stanley Downe at the scene and identify him as actively participating in the theft of the processed pot, the notorious drug of marijuana. He was obviously the mastermind of the plan and the ringleader of the gang, due to his foreknowledge. We will, Milord, establish *mens rea*. Stanley Downe is entirely accountable for his own actions, plus those of other accomplices under his command."

Phil Figgwiggin's client was allowed to vacate the prisoner's box and sit next to Phil at the defence table so they might more conveniently confer during the trial. Mike Fowler was right behind them in the public pews. He'd agreed to act as Phil's gofer as needed.

Phil rose to present his opening address. Two well-dressed dowagers in the public gallery swooned, causing some delay, as they had to be helped from the courtroom.

"Let's get one topic both on and off the table at the start," Phil began. "My learned friend seeks to use various erroneous arguments, referring to marijuana as an evil and notorious drug. Perhaps I should put pot in perspective. It is a far less dangerous substance than alcohol, which is a vast and perfectly legal industry almost everywhere on the planet. For thousands of years, the hemp plant and its byproducts were also legal and in use all over the world.

"However, the centres of power now responsible for the control of drugs are the same centres disseminating the artificial hysteria necessary for the continued criminalization of marijuana, in order that they themselves can continue to profit therefrom. That is what keeps the retail price of pot a hundred times higher than its natural value, and keeps the trade exclusively in the hands of the so-called criminal element.

"The law blocks every initiative for reform of this misguided drug policy. Too many people are making money from the trade, including governments, politicians, police, and other law enforcement groups and intelligence agencies in the USA, such as the CIA and the DEA. That is why there is no reform of a drug policy that upholds the dogma of prohibition and repression. And they keep this secretive business safe and lucrative by placing it in the hands of illegal drug traffickers. The War on Drugs is an unmitigated, hypocritical farce. It is a propaganda trick that causes more suffering from drugs than it prevents.

"Now to the specifics of this case, Milord. What is alleged to have been stolen in this case, and what is theft? Everyone commits theft, who, fraudulently and without colour of right, takes or converts to his own use, anything, whether animate or inanimate, with intent to deprive the owner of the thing. The pot that the Crown seeks to say was stolen, by whomever it was who did or did not do so, was on its way to being completely destroyed in an incinerator, by those in possession thereof, the police themselves. Can we even say they were the owners? It had no value in their eyes. QED, they had nothing in their possession of any value when it was taken from them.

"That they refused to give the pot away rather than burn it is to their discredit; especially when one considers that the police themselves had obtained this substance from the real and previous owners by force.

"Note the use of the word 'anything,' Milord, in Section 322 of the Criminal Code. It is not anything that is alleged to have been stolen in the present case; it is nothing.

"Whoever it was who actually saved this plant product from destruction – and this has naught to do with my client – far from taking anything of value from rightful owners, was obviously merely intent on recycling same. Is it not possible, therefore, that whoever took it should be lauded rather than prosecuted, as they are contributors to the gross national product, not destroyers thereof. Waste not, want not is an expression often heard, and one that is not without considerable merit.

"I suggest we hear no more from the prosecution, who would attempt to render this charge more serious than it already is, in a case that should be reduced, Milord, to a minor case of assault, a mere altercation over nothing of value. This is not a case of theft over $5,000, or under $5,000, but a difference of opinion arising between two parties, one wishing to destroy a useful natural plant byproduct, the other, an environmental group, wishing to conserve same."

Novark nearly broke an ankle jumping to his feet to voice a strenuous objection. "This is ridiculous, Milord. My learned friend is attempting to impose some sort of subjective and nebulous attribute on a criminal substance with a known high street value, and we will produce evidence to that effect!"

Figgwiggin was quick to reply. "The substance in question would only have high street value if it were to be sold by its RCMP owners, something they did not intend to do, by their own actions and admission. I'm prepared to admit that if the constabulary were to sell pot, or if they used it themselves, then the substance would acquire a value. Is the

Crown able or willing to produce evidence that the Mounties have sold or used pot at any time? I don't think they are able or willing to do so. Therefore, it has no value to them."

"Neither of those scenarios is a matter of RCMP policy," said Novark, "and you know it. I submit that the pot is temporarily in RCMP custody until they legally destroy same. The case is crystal clear. My learned friend is attempting to throw the baby out the window with the bathwater, to inject slippery legal dictums into the mix in order to confuse the issue before the court."

"So you say," Phil interjected, "and well said, I must admit, but then just who is the owner? I would be prepared to cross-examine on and argue that subject if necessary. Furthermore, and most importantly, Milord, the Crown has not found anything in the possession of my client. Naught, nada, nil!"

Justice Hoverdaire stirred. "Are we to presume that no Mounties have ever partaken of or sold pot in their possession, or that some Mounties may very well have done so, as could be the possible conclusion in this case?" he asked. "In the former instance, which I am presuming would be the outcome of any questioning of the RCMP on that subject, the legal question would then become whether anything of no value in the hands of an owner can be the object of theft when the persons who are in possession of it are deprived of same. Semantics, perhaps.

"I'll take these matters under advisement. Come back after the recess prepared to argue the point and it will be my duty to smooth the asperities of litigation. Court is adjourned till this afternoon at two o'clock, at which time we shall proceed forthwith, or later, if not with the most possible delay."

"What in hell did he mean by that?" Stan whispered to Phil as they rose for the adjournment.

"He meant that when the chips are down and the last dog's being shot, who's on top?" Phil replied.

"So, did we win that round?" asked Stan.

"Not likely, but that will get Novark overconfident while we set him up for the sucker punch."

Doggerel Don had by this point clobbered together the beginnings of a poem:

"Order in court," the clerk calls out and further says, "All rise."
The judge, Justice Hugo Hoverdaire, is the subject of all eyes
He hunches his robes, sits on the bench indicating it's time to commence
He nods at the two learned counsels, representing the crown and defence
The learned Philip Figgwiggin, QC, counsel for the defence
He has the role of challenging all, boldly without pretence
The evidence of the prosecution, then with exculpatory
Evidence of his own, present a conflicting story.

One that casts doubt on the Crown assertion that Stan Downe is the one
He would challenge the authenticity of what had been said he had done
No turn would be left unstoned, no aspersions left unremarked
He would shred all the Crown's assertions, in the trashcan they'd be parked

The audience takes in the scene, was justice to be served?
What would be the outcome is something that would be observed.
The first to speak would be Joe Novark, then his learned friend
Philip Figgwiggin would invoke his skill his client to defend.

Bait and Switch

Since her narrow escape from *durance vile,* Thistle had become interested in legal proceedings and had taken to attending trials at the Victoria courthouse. She was eager to see her legal saviour in action, and was contemplating a career on the correct side of the law. Phil Figgwiggin had certainly encouraged her to consider that option.

Thistle was particularly interested in Stan Downe's trial. She was seated in an ideal position to observe Constable Downe when two security officers brought him into the courtroom. *My God, I'm looking at Neale!* They made eye contact, but there was no reaction on his part, and she realized they had never met before. Thistle avidly followed the morning's events, and only regretted missing a chance to tell Figgwiggin how impressive his performance had been.

After the break, the clerk re-opened court at two sharp. Mr. Justice Hoverdaire leaned forward to address Novark: "I presume you intend to impugn Mr. Figgwiggin's argument regarding the ownership and value of the pot." At Novark's statement in the affirmative, Hoverdaire said, "Proceed."

"Milord, I refer the court to section 328 of the Code. I

maintain that the Crown in the form of the RCMP had a special de facto property or interest in the narcotic in question, which existed at the time the theft was committed. I would refer to *R. v Smith*, (1962), S.C.R. 215, 131 C.C.C., 403 and 36 C.RR. 834. On the facts that will be presented, the accused deprived the Crown of that special property or interest.

"In *R. v Scallen* (1974), 15 C.C.C. (2d), 441 (B.C.C.A.), it was held that the word 'anything' in that section of the Code was wide enough to include bank credit and that 'anything' need not be something tangible or material. As pot is both tangible and material, the word would seem to cover the point only too clearly.

"I would also draw the court's attention to *R. v Pace*, (1965) 3 C.C.C. 55, 48 D.LR. (2d) 532 (N.S.C.A.), which states that theft may still be committed though the object is of no use or value to the owner. The evidence that is adduced by the Crown reasonably identifies the owner with the personage named in the indictment as owner. Even if that were regarded as lacking in precision, it would not mislead or prejudice the accused in the preparation or presentation of his defence. I rest my argument on that point."

"What have you to say in reply, Mr. Figgwiggin?" asked the judge.

"Only this, Milord, which I add to my previous argument. To come within the term 'anything' as it is used in the Code, the thing which is taken, whether tangible or intangible, must be such that it can be the subject of a proprietary right and the property must be capable of being taken or converted in a manner that results in the deprivation of the victim. The police were not victims, and they did not own anything that was of any value to them. So how can anything be stolen from them?

"That is as succinctly as I can put it, Milord, and that is my contention in the unusual circumstances that are involved in this case. I await your decision with great respect on the point, with the de rigeur bated breath, ever hopeful of a decision in my favour."

Hoverdaire replied, "I did some research of my own and, having heard legal argument from learned counsel in the matter, I hereby render my decision on a point of some difficulty. The police had a sufficient proprietary interest to constitute ownership in the thing that was stolen from them, a thing that had very considerable value to the thieves, likely in excess of $5,000. Now, let's get on with the trial. Mr. Novark, call your first witness."

Phil turned in his seat and gave a signal to Mike Fowler, who got up and left the courtroom.

Prosecutor Novark complied with the judge's request, putting his star witness, Joe Kerr, the one witness critical to the offence charged, on the stand. Kerr was sworn in and, with step-by-step prompting from the prosecutor, gave his version of the events surrounding the robbery. This took some time, as the Crown was determined to build an unassailable case against the accused.

"Do you see the same man here today, the man you know as a fellow police officer, the man whom you saw at the scene of the crime, the man who attacked and robbed you?" Novark asked.

"Yes, I do."

"Would you point him out, please?"

Constable Kerr indicated Stan Downe.

"I will call your partner next," said Novark, "and he can speak for himself; but would Constable John Potts have been in a position to also observe the accused?"

"Certainly not to the extent that I did. I got a full-face view, while John was much farther away, engaged in a struggle with another of the thieves, but he might have caught a fleeting glimpse."

"No further questions," said Novark, and took his seat.

Stan Downe knew how damning Kerr's testimony was. He whispered in Phil's ear, and Phil rose. "My client is in need of a bathroom break," he advised the court. "May I have a short adjournment before beginning my cross-examination of this witness?"

"Granted," said Justice Hugo Hoverdaire. "This is as good a time as any for a short recess."

The security guards accompanied Stan Downe to the men's washroom and stood outside the door while he went in.

Mike Fowler and Neale Downe were already inside, occupying cubicles. On Stan's entry, the identical twins began exchanging clothes. In less than two minutes they had completed the task, while Mike stood at the entrance to stall the security guards if either should suddenly decide to enter cannery row. Neale had prepared by adopting the same haircut as Stan, based on Mike's description. Neale emerged from the washroom checking his fly and accompanied the two guards back into the courtroom.

A few steps in, he looked across the room and there was Florence, the girl he had longed to find again. Neale broke into a wide grin. Thistle smiled back, then sat down in a quandary. What kind of ackamaracka is going on here? she wondered.

Neale said nothing and took his seat next to Phil at the counsel table.

A few minutes later, Stan also came out of the men's room, clad in Neale's clothes and a slouch hat. As the trial recommenced, he slipped unobtrusively into the back row of the public gallery, keeping his head down. He stashed the hat under the seat.

Phil rose to cross-examine Kerr. No women fainted, but several got their knickers in a twist.

"You say you found yourself in a desperate fight with several opponents?" asked Phil.

"Yes, one man and two women." Joe answered.

"And this all happened very suddenly?"

"Yes. One minute I was trying to help one of the women with her car and the next thing, all hell broke loose."

"You weren't expecting it?"

"No."

"Then I put it to you that you were in a disordered state

of chaotic confusion at this unexpected assault on your person."

Joe had been well rehearsed. "You can't put it to me. You're only supposed to ask me questions."

Justice Hoverdaire interjected, "The witness is correct, Mr. Figgwiggin. So let's not have anymore put-it-to-you's in your cross-examination, please."

"Certainly, Milord." Figgwiggin stared at the witness for a moment, then said, "You stated that you knew Stan Downe as a fellow officer in the RCMP, and that when you tore off your assailant's mask, you immediately recognized him to be that person?"

"Yes."

"Your testimony-in-chief did not indicate that you spoke to him. So if you recognized Stan, why didn't you say anything to him? Something like, 'Fancy meeting you here,' for instance?"

"I didn't get the chance. Stan punched me in the stomach and then in the face. One of the women slapped a pad of chloroform across my face. After that, I was out of action."

"Are you certain that the man you saw was Stan Downe?"

"Positive!"

"If given the chance, then, you would also know Stan Downe by talking to him about things only you and he would know about, relating to your association as police officers?"

"Of course."

Phil turned to the gallery. "I would ask Constable Stan Downe to come down here in front of the witness so that he might have a better look at him and talk to him if he so desires."

Various gasps and cries emanated from both the gallery and prosecution table as a man came forward out of the public gallery and stood before the court. "Take a good look at him," Phil said to Joe. "Talk to him. Is this Constable Stan Downe or not? Take your time."

Justice Hoverdaire pounded his gavel. "Order in the court! What's going on here?"

Phil signaled for Neale Downe to stand up before the court as well, and asked loudly of the witness in the box, pointing at Neale, "Or is this the man who attacked you? Or is it either of them, for that matter?"

The two men were dead ringers. Kerr was banjaxed. Novark was apoplectic and began yelling, "I object! Foul play!" The peanut gallery was abuzz with conjecture, but delighted to be getting their money's worth.

"Be careful, Mr. Figgwiggin," said Justice Hugo. "You're straying too close to being out of order here."

"Not so, Milord. With all due respect, I am only trying to demonstrate the frailties associated with eyewitness testimony. Said testimony can be notoriously unreliable, and certainly is in this case. A fact that I particularly wish Your Lordship to note.

"The prosecution cannot rely on fleeting and inaccurate evidence of identification. They cannot prove their case beyond a reasonable doubt, and certainly not when they have found no stolen property in the possession of the accused."

"Who is this other man who stands before us?" asked the judge. "He's a doppelganger if I ever saw one."

"Does it really matter? Actually, Milord, he is Neale Downe, the twin brother of Stan Downe."

"And why shouldn't I cite him for contempt of court or some such charge for pulling a switcheroo like this? To say nothing of yourself, Mr. Figgwiggin, because I don't think you're an innocent bystander in this little vaudeville skit. You have to be guilty of some breach of court procedure."

"Milord, may I suggest that it is a legal presumption that counsel always know what they're doing in the course of seeking justice?"

"I'm adjourning the trial for the moment, and I want to see you and Mr. Novark in my chambers in five minutes."

"Of course."

Novark was fulminating, mouthing objections and

pounding the table. Phil whipped over to the prosecution table and grabbed him by the arm.

"Listen carefully, Joan, because I shall tell you this only once," he said in his ear. "The judge is going to have to dismiss the case and you know it – on the grounds of possible mistaken identity. Don't sweat it; the cops aren't going to criticize you. They'll be ecstatic over an acquittal, as a matter of fact. It exonerates the Force. You must realize that they didn't really want one of their own to be found guilty of theft. Now they're off the hook. So quit objecting. Let's get in there and placate the judge."

Phil and Mike exchanged a hug and a blackslap. "Well, I'll be a dirty-word," said Mike. "Don't that just beat all, we rang in a humdinger of a ringer. Hot diggety damn!"

Turning toward the spectators, they saw Neale and Thistle locked in an embrace, kissing feverishly.

When Your Heart's on Fire

Wanda Fucah marched into Phil's office, holding an envelope aloft. "Look what just arrived in the mail."

"What?" asked Figgwiggin, looking up from the file on his desk.

"A cheque for ten thousand dollars."

"And rightly so."

Wanda planted a hand on her hip. "Don't act so blasé. You lawyers are just like rhinoceroses."

"What do you mean by that?"

"You're thick-skinned, short-sighted and always willing to charge."

Figgwiggin smiled. He couldn't imagine running his office without old irascible Wanda. "Who's the cheque from?"

"Neale Downe. He's paid both his and Thistle Fielgud's bill, even though you offered to take her case for free, you sentimental old fool. Guess that means those two are more than just an item now."

"Just shows to go you. Cast your bread on the legal waters and it doesn't always come back soggy and unfit to eat!"

"This takes care of your overdraft and then some," she said, handing him the envelope. "What do you intend to do with it? Bearing in mind what a hard-working eager beaver I am."

"Point taken. I'm leaving Sunday for Seabreeze. Mike's been going back and forth collecting their goods, and I promised to give him a hand. I'll stay for a few days, get in some R & R while he and Evelyn wrap things up there."

Phil waved Wanda into a seat, then leaned back in his chair. "I've been talking to Mike about using him as an unofficial investigator and researcher."

"Great idea," Wanda enthused. "He sure had a ball helping you with the Neale and Stan switcheroo."

Figgwiggin nodded, stroking his goatee. "Yes, he's fearless and he's great with people. He'd spice up the team, and he'd have a little extra retirement income."

"Even if he turns you down, with him living in the same condo, you'll at least have a new pal, someone to bounce your ideas off. In addition to my wise counsel, of course."

They met at the corner of Cook and Fairfield Road as arranged, and walked arm in arm down chestnut-lined Cook Street toward the village. Thistle came clean with Neale about her former life.

To her surprise and delight, he simply said, "Florence – I mean Thistle – we all have a past. I'm in no position to judge you or anyone else. But if you'll agree, I think we could be very happy together, and that's all that matters to me."

In a moment of commitment phobia, Thistle blurted, "In my experience, all men want is sex, and they don't much care where they get it."

"I guess my mother felt the same way," Neale mused. "Once when I was about four, she came into the bathroom to wash my back and caught me playing with my testicles.

"'Are these my brains, Mommy?' I asked her. She thought for a second while she soaped up the washcloth. 'Not yet,' she said."

Thistle burst into laughter, then quietly asked, "Are you sure about us, Neale?"

"Absolutely. And now it's my turn to talk about the past so it doesn't affect our future." Grinning, he added, "Hemp me, I wanna go straight."

"As long as you don't meth around, and as long as you help me, too. Then there'll be no methadone in our madness for each other."

"Enough with the drug puns," Neale said, laughing. Sobering, he added, "I want you to know, I was never into hard drugs at all. Never used them, never dealt them. I used to say, A friend in need is a pest, get rid of him; but a friend with weed is a friend indeed."

"Same here," said Thistle. "Only used mariweegee."

They had walked as far as the Beagle Pub. "Shall we go in and have a drink?" asked Neale wryly.

"I've got a better idea. Let's go to my place. It's near here, in a garret apartment in a house," she said loftily. "Phil's a great guy; he arranged it for me. I'm baby-sitting the whole house while the owners are on holiday."

"Good idea," Neale answered.

"When we get there, maybe we could play around," Thistle said skittishly.

"Another good idea. But keep in mind that we have to blow this town. I figure those Mounties still want to nail me to a cross for that pot heist, or anything else they can think of.

"That prosecutor's madder than a cut snake, too. He'll have a hair up his arse until he figures out a way to lay some kind of charge against me. And I don't plan to go into the clink. You want to come along?" Neale asked straightforwardly.

"Better not leave without me," Thistle replied receptively.

They arrived at the door of a white two-storey Edwardian house on Moss Street, two blocks up from the bluffs overlooking Juan de Fuca Strait.

Entering the house through the foyer, Neale noticed a well-appointed living room complete with piano.

"Shall I play the piano for you?" Thistle asked grandly.

"Can you play in tune?"

"No," Thistle answered flatly. "This isn't my part of the house, so why not come up to my room and make a different kind of music?" she added invitingly.

They went upstairs and entered the bedroom.

Thistle purred seductively, placing her hand on his chest.

"I've always wanted to make love to you," he said with rising excitement, "but I've got to go to the bathroom first," Neale stalled.

"It's right over there," Thistle said cannily, flicking on the light for him.

"I won't be long," Neale pithily replied.

He came out flushed.

"I think I'll take off my dress," she said silkily.

"You have a gorgeous body," he said as he watched her undress. "Let me remove your bra," he snapped.

"All right," she said, making a clean breast of things.

Moving closer to him, Thistle ran her fingers along Neale's chest, then lightly raked her nails over the exposed skin above the top button of his shirt. He shivered.

Hugging her close, Neale said, "How about I arrange two tickets to Timbuktu? They'll never find us there."

"Sounds good. We can both start fresh with someone who shares and cares. But what are we going to use for money? Remember, you had to pay my legal fees. "

"No problem. I'm loaded with lolly, and I have no intention of giving it back. We'll stop off in the Cymans to pick up some long green from my bank account. I've paid off a few friends – I don't like the word accomplices, it makes everyone sound guilty – so after a holiday, all we have to worry about is finding somewhere to settle down."

"A place with some opportunities."

"That reminds me, I really should send Phil Figgwiggin

another ten thousand while we're gone. You and I wouldn't
even know each other if it hadn't been for him."

"We could have ended up in the same jail!" Thistle exclaimed.

"But not in the same cell."

"That much togetherness would never work," Thistle
agreed.

Taking him by the hand, she added, "Things don't mean
much without someone to share them with. Why don't you
take off your trousers now?" she panted.

His shaking hands slid the garment to the floor, along
with his boxers. "You have a gorgeous body, too," she said
figuratively.

"I'm all set," he declared cockily. He pulled her to him.

"I'm ready, too," she said receptively. They fell onto the
bed. After much groping and thrashing, Neale drove his
point home.

"Am I in deep enough?" he asked penetratingly.

"Yes," she moaned movingly.

"Yeeeeyouugh!" Neale ejaculated.

"Ohhhhhhh!" Thistle climaxed.

They stayed in the hay all night, doing the nine ways
that could save your life: horizontal jogging, bush patrol, a
dash in the bloomers, parallel parking, hiding the salami,
ploughing the back forty, spearing the bearded clam, wham
bam, thank you ma'am, banging like an outhouse door in a
gale.

As they fell back, exhausted, watching the dawn enter
through Thistle's window, both of them were aware of the
risks facing an ex-prostitute and a dope dealer on the lam.
But when your heart's on fire, smoke gets in your eyes.

ADDENDUM

There are few laughs in this addendum, unless you think the war on cannabis is a joke.

One day, while purchasing a mocha latte at a coffee shop in Victoria, BC, I noticed two elderly ladies wearing red jackets with *Crime Watch – Volunteer* emblazoned on the back and front. I was writing a novel involving the decriminalization of marijuana, so I struck up a conversation with them.

"Do you find there's any significant amount of marijuana dealing or smoking around the village?" I asked. They invited me to sit at their table.

"Not that we've noticed," the smaller of the two said. Her snow-white hair haloed her delicate face and her tiny frame swam inside the bulky jacket.

"What kind of crime do you watch for?" I asked. "A criminal is only a person who's been caught committing a dishonest deed but can't afford a good lawyer, or one who hasn't sufficient capital to form a corporation. Do you see any such people here today?"

The taller woman said, "It's hard to tell. We just wear these jackets to convey the impression to criminals that they're being watched."

"There's a crime going on right now," I pointed out.

"What crime?"

They both glanced around the café.

"The price of these lattes! Now, let me ask you ladies, are you in favour of decriminalizing marijuana?"

"No," was the emphatic joint reply.

"Why not?"

"Because it will lead innocent people to use harder drugs," the taller one said.

"Are you sure? Holding hands can sometimes lead to fornication, but not as often as one would like."

"You're being facetious, my good man," she replied with a sniff. "I don't know that we're entirely appreciative –"

"You *do* know why Baptists don't make love standing up?" I continued.

She bit. "Why not?"

"Because it may lead to dancing! Do you ladies want to try some pot? That way you'll know what you're dealing with. I could get some and you could test your reaction."

"I don't smoke," Snow White said, and her companion shook her head vigorously.

"We'll put it in brownies."

"I didn't know you could do that," said Snow White, "but I'd rather have a drink of scotch."

"You do know that alcohol or tobacco are ten times more addictive than cannabis?"

Well, that was the end of the conversation, as the ladies pleaded pressing engagements elsewhere and left.

There is a criminal conspiracy at work against the hemp plant and its derivatives. The so-called War on Drugs has cost US taxpayers $70 billion a year, and close to a trillion dollars over the past 35 years. Figures in Canada are likely similar. Yet drugs remain cheaper and more available today.

If marijuana enjoyed the same legal status as alcohol, people would be able to grow it commercially and sell it in government-licensed stores. It would be subject to health and quality controls and taxes, and it wouldn't have to be more expensive than other plant products.

What does our Conservative government of Canada plan to do about marijuana? On November 20, 2007, it unveiled legislation calling for a mandatory six-month jail term for people convicted of trafficking in illicit drugs, including those who grow only a single plant.

The new bill proposes a two-year mandatory term for running a marijuana-growing operation of 500 plants or more. It also calls for a doubling of the maximum prison term for cannabis production, from seven to fourteen years.

"We want to put organized crime out of business," said Justice Minister Rob Nicholson when the legislation was tabled.

"You can never beat organized crime as long as you have prohibition," countered Marc Emery, Vancouver's famous "Prince of Pot."

Which of those statements makes more sense?

Years of criminalization have failed. Gangs have prospered from it, and in fact, they've flourished and expanded.

The definition of insanity is to keep doing the same stupid things over and over again. Instead of lending de facto support to organized crime, Prime Minister Stephen Harper and other MPs who back the new law should get mandatory jail sentences for aiding and abetting the drug trade.

But the electorate should also take appropriate action at the ballot box, by electing members with the ability to properly analyze the problem.

Jean Chretien was the first Canadian politician to suggest decriminalizing marijuana. The subsequent Le Dain Commission of 1969 to 1973 recommended ending criminal charges for marijuana possession. When the commission's report came out, the US Drug Enforcement Administration (DEA) applied tremendous political pressure on Canada not to legalize marijuana, and of course we folded like a circus tent.

And that brings us to law enforcement agencies and others who might be out of work if grass were made legal. They should know by now that it's the law itself that causes the bootlegging of the product and the crime.

Canada's estimated 215,000 marijuana grow-ops employ more than half a million people. These individuals have a vested interest in the present system, which keeps the price high and their grow-ops very profitable. Some 1.8 million British Colombians, a majority of the province's adult population, say they've used marijuana. The industry generates six billion dollars in annual sales, placing it just behind forestry and tourism as an economic force in BC.

As long as demand is strong and the public considers marijuana use acceptable, the supply will be there. It's a sort of civil war, users and peddlers versus police and the justice system, while the taxpayer pays the cost.

There are currently 2,735 inmates in provincial jail and

eighty percent them are double bunked. If mandatory sentencing for pot trafficking is enacted, BC's already crowded jails will have to squeeze in hundreds, if not thousands, of marijuana growers per year. The province is going to need new prisons.

Maybe we'll also follow the US example and privatize the building of prisons. Somebody's going to make a lot of money on that bit of business.

If alcohol was deemed too dangerous to be left in the hands of organized crime, then the same judgment should apply to marijuana.

By 1900, nearly four generations of North Americans had been using cannabis, and doctors had been prescribing cannabis extract medications even to children and presidents. At the time, physicians didn't consider the substance habit-forming, nor its users prone to violent or otherwise anti-social behaviour.

World's fairs and international expositions of the period often featured hashish-smoking concessions, and were extremely popular among fairgoers. In the 1880s, the *Police Gazette* estimated there were over 500 smoking parlours in New York City; they were still there in the 1920s. By then, the city boasted more hashish parlours than speakeasies.

Hemp, a most profitable crop and a viable substitute for paper made from wood pulp, could have saved our forests. It still can. One acre of hemp can replace 4.1 acres of trees, and it can be grown anywhere.

In 1931, Harry J. Anslinger, America's Assistant Commissioner for Prohibition, became director of the new Federal Bureau of Narcotics, the DEA's predecessor. At Congressional hearings on drugs in 1937, Anslinger cited as fact and read aloud the yellow journalism and rantings of William Randolph Hearst and others with forestry interests, who stood to lose market share to hemp.

Anslinger, who couldn't come within shouting distance of the truth, was chief apologist for Senator Joseph McCarthy, whom he secretly – and illegally – supplied with morphine for years, ostensibly so the communists couldn't blackmail McCarthy for his drug dependency.

The first step toward the prohibition of hemp and its derivatives was to introduce the fear of the unknown, by using a term no one had ever heard of before: marijuana. In addition, most of the hearings were held behind closed doors, to thwart potential defenders of hemp.

Tapping into an existing pool of racial hatred that was already poisoning American society in the 1930s, black entertainers' jazz and swing music were declared to be the outgrowth of marijuana use.

Yet when the Japanese attacked Pearl Harbour and cut off the supply of Manila hemp from the Philippines, the US government produced the film Hemp for Victory, to encourage farmers to grow the crop for the war effort. When hostilities ended, the ban on hemp went back into effect.

During the Inquisition, the Roman Catholic Church declared cannabis an unholy sacrament in Satanic masses. Healers who used the plant medicinally were branded as heretics and witches and, along with hundreds of thousands of other "sinners," put to death following lengthy torture. Inquisitors then divided up the heretics' forfeited property. The individual who denounced you got a third of your property, another third went to the government and the remainder went to the papacy.

Medical experts today hail marijuana's physiological benefits, including chronic pain relief and fever reduction, and the plant's ability to soothe aching muscles and ease childbirth.

As Jim Hackler, University of Victoria criminology professor, says in his book, Canadian Criminology Strategies and Perspectives, "If one were to use harm to human beings as a reason for making substances illegal, alcohol (and tobacco) would certainly rank higher on the scale of undesirable substances than those which are currently illegal. . .For illicit drugs, the major harms seem to arise from the fact that they are illegal."

Any recreational use of cannabis could never come close to matching the harm done by alcohol or cigarettes. Habitual users of pot may not become any smarter, but all the alcoholics I ever knew are now dead.

Proud Canadian Hal Sisson was born in Moose Jaw, Saskatchewan. His varied career includes a stint as a reporter
for the *Saskatoon Star-Phoenix* and a thirty-year law practice
in Alberta's Peace River country. While there, he got involved
in provincial politics and conceived, produced and starred in
Western Canada's longest-running burlesque revue. Sisson is
a former ranking Canadian and US player of six-wicket USCA
and international croquet, and remains an avid collector of
marbles. Now a resident of Victoria, BC, Sisson helped launch
that city's chapter of the 9/11 Truth Movement. He continues
to write non-fiction books and novels, Potshots being his elev-
enth title. Fans can visit Hal's website at:

www.halsisson.ca

Get these other great Sisson titles!

Modus Operandi 9/11   0-9731109-2-9
What really brought down the Twin Towers and sparked the war in Iraq? A tale driven by passion and humour in equal measure.

Sorry 'Bout That   1-59526-493-0
Sisson's affectionate tribute to twenty years as producer and star of Western Canada's longest-running burlesque revue.

Coots, Codgers and Curmudgeons 1-894012-04-6
Garage Sale of the Mind   1-894012-07-0
Two hilarious compilations of short stories from the salty duo of Hal Sisson and Dwayne Rowe.

Caverns of the Cross   1-55152-049-4
A Canadian scientist develops a natural contraceptive from native Brazilian flora. Agents of the Vatican and powerful pharmaceutical companies will stop at nothing, not even murder, to control the formula and set the course of society.

A Fat Lot of Good   1-894012-06-2
Armed with nitro spray and cheeky wit, senior sleuths Figgwiggin and Fowler close in on the killer of a cardiologist.

Maquiladora Mayhem   1-894012-08-9
Figgwiggin and Fowler head for Mexico's maquiladora zone to battle the arcane forces of the New World Order.

You Should Live So Long   1-894012-09-7
Superannuated sleuths Figgwiggin and Fowler are out to foil a murder plot against Mother Earth.

The Big Bamboozle   1-894012-03-8
Great ape Bamboo is kidnapped from his jungle home and sold to a Toronto zoo, and becomes an advocate for the fight to save species from extinction.

Order Form

PHONE with credit card, toll-free in North America: 1-888-713-8500, or from overseas: 1-705-728-6500. FAX this page with credit card info to: 1-8788-713-8883, from overseas to: 1-705-728-6500. SURF to our secure Web store at www.GlobalOutlook.ca and use PayPal, Mastercard or VISA. Or you can MAIL this form and your credit card info, cheque or money order in US funds to:

Global Outlook, PO Box 222, Oro, Ontario, Canada, L0L 2X0

Please add $6.00 (Canadian or US) for shipping and handling for first book, $2.00 more for each additional book.

Modus Operandi 9/11	($11 CAD/$10 US)	_____
Sorry 'Bout That	($22 CAD/$20 US)	_____
Coots, Codgers and Curmudgeons	($16 CAD/$15 US)	_____
Garage Sale of the Mind	($16 CAD/$15 US)	_____
Caverns of the Cross	($16 CAD/$15 US)	_____
A Fat Lot of Good	($11 CAD/$10 US)	_____
Maquiladora Mayhem	($11 CAD/$10 US)	_____
You Should Live So Long	($11 CAD/$10 US)	_____
The Big Bamboozle	($11 CAD/$10 US)	_____

Subtotal $ _____ + S & H $ _____ = $ _____ Enclosed

Name: _____

Address: _____

_____

E-mail: _____

Phone: _____

VISA/MC #: _____

Expiry (MM/YY: _____

Above prices subject to change without notice.